ABRUPT

by

william a luckey

ABRUPT

Cover photo by Belinda Perry

Published in 2016

For more information about William A.
Luckey, please go to waluckey-west.com.
sajaluckey@gmail.com to contact the author

William A. Luckey

Dedicated to my brother, his family, all the children, his and mine, nieces and nephews and grandchildren of all shapes and sizes

With special thanks to Sarah 'Bees' Harvey for her amazing talent

ABRUPT

OTHER BOOKS BY WILLIAM LUCKEY

Here it was. Far as he could go. The end of his step-by-step travels. He could only stand, draw air through his lung in gasps, let the air slowly fill his lungs, then breathe out. Hope it was enough to keep him upright and alert.

Looking at what surrounded him, he could guess at the life lived here. Each place had become familiar since he'd drifted around the country, using back roads and accepting few rides, tired now and uncertain. He'd learned to take what came his way with few questions.

Unintentional rock rested in scattered lumps, secure for a hundred years; few stones had rolled from their tight beginning on the ground to lie exposed and defenseless on flattened grass, mute witness to separation. Rocks had been thrown into gullies, meant to stop erosion, maintain a semblance of flat surface that could carry a car or truck, or could balance a horse and wagon without unexpected deep wallows.

He sat on a flat table-sized rock. No choice, no grace or control, helpless to continue his self-chosen journey. The stone beneath him appeared to have been selected for comfort, to cradle the lean buttocks of an unwitting traveler, offering the illusion of welcome to the weary or dispossessed.

There had been countless years of walking, resting, working when possible. Reading the land, seeing similar patterns in odd parts of the country; stone walls grew where rock was abundant and the land fertile. Dirt and washouts, deeper gullies, grew wide and restless when grass, weeds, and rain were sparse.

His head rested in his hands, elbows braced on his thighs. In front of him, across the road and set back, there were the remains of a farm; burnt and broken hardware seemed familiar. Unnerving.

He knew the more ominous signs; exhaustion, hard breathing, bad omens for any man, worse for a drifter carrying within him a private and imminent destruction.

His body was slowly coming undone. No magic, no pills or prescriptions; that's what he'd been told. Don't do much, be careful, be mindful of what waited for him. Nothing more than anyone could expect from life, except that in his case the moment could and would come unexpected and too soon.

Hell, he thought. Even love-making or sex or whatever happened between men and women could kill him.

He'd tried, more often than literally was good for him. Made him almost laugh at what he could and didn't know. Take away women and there wasn't much for a man, except that each moment was a gift, small or large, and he intended to enjoy what might be possible.

The stone beneath his bony rump had begun to bother him, which meant he'd sat long enough and it was time. Standing up, as usual, was a difficult move, one he knew took time and burned an energy he could ill-afford. But he intended to stand. And walk. Until something to eat showed up, or a sweet-smelling barn where he could sleep after a brief wash, a drink of well water. Then blessed sleep.

"MARTIN, WHO'S THAT?" Down the road some, she thought, no one walks out here. "Martin!" The farm woman yelled at her husband, wanting his answer to confirm what she suspected. A bum, setting right outside on that old dug-up stone that was off the trail and out of the way. At least this drifter looked too darn tired to cause trouble.

"Martin!" That stoic man, habitually reluctant to answer. Why she could be attacked right here in her own kitchen and her sworn husband might turn around from a chore and wonder why she'd been calling him.

"Martin!!"

He was slow to respond, since he too had been studying the man and thought there was something familiar, something he couldn't quite name, and Irene's demanding voice was driving out the edge of an old memory that Martin wanted to ponder.

"I see him, old woman. He won't bother us none." That should quiet her. Martin watched as the hiker stood very carefully and seemed to be breathing hard. The air was dry and clear, easy enough to see the man's chest rise and fall, hesitate then rise again. Martin shook his head.

Couldn't quite put a name to the tired man, then again it's been some years since he'd might have seen this one, and time could be hard on a man, changing him from a gawky youngster to the wreck that appeared outside the door and down the road a safe distance.

Martin remembered the name finally; hadn't seen much of him, just when the boy and his pa came to market. He was surprised; boy wasn't meant to last, ran away when he was in his teens, pa'd said the boy enlisted but there'd never been his name on any list.

"Irene you hush now. I'm going to ask him. He's movin' slow, won't take more'n a bit of hurry to catch up."

A FEW STEPS and his muscles came together. Henry Lawson recognized the stuttered movements meant to knit him and form a unit that, on occasion could be capable of surprising strength.

The land was familiar yet different, he could have passed through here before. Some houses new, a few going back past the present century. Barns, sheds, rusted machinery broken windows. Barren spots, a low foundation, burned scrub and charred tree trunks, evidence of what teased Henry even as he could not bring to his tired mind what memories waited for him.

Behind him a form approached; a grown man using a cane to balance hurried steps. Words drifted past but Henry had no thought to link them together.

"Hey, you. Yes you. Slow down let me catch my breath. You, boy. Goddamn it stop"

SHE WATCHED FROM the kitchen window. There was Martin again, hurrying to catch up to a bum, a no-good drifter and even from this distance she could tell her husband was apologizing as he chased the man down. The bum finally stopped, Martin slid by then turned on his cane and faced the man.

Two men, close enough, seen through Irene's judgmental eyes. The drifter was lean, like those whose meals came too far apart and lacked even casual nutrition. The stranger was young against Martin's years, no surprise there. Martin was her life-long love and companion; short and once strong, white hair light enough the slightest wind moved it and as usual Martin didn't seem to care

In comparing these two, Irene could not help but favor her Martin. Perhaps not the brightest of the bunch but always at heart a good man.

Irene couldn't hear but she could guess. Martin was slow working up to what was important. While she waited, Irene studied the drifter. Boy was taller when he straightened up. Weren't no boy either. Age and time had thinned his face, took away what might have been decent looks and left him plain, and tired, perhaps even ill. She surely didn't want him in her home.

While Martin talked, the drifter took that durned hat off, rolled the brim in his long fingers. Hands banged up some, face soiled, darkened along the jaw with a poor excuse for a beard. Eyes might be light colored, she couldn't tell from where she stood, but the hair was broken gray and needed trimmin'.

Martin said something displeasing and the bum dropped his head, wiped a filthy hand over his eyes. Irene dried her hands on a towel, smoothed the front of her housecoat and stepped outside. Up to her, she'd set these two men straight, so she and Martin could get back to their Sunday chores.

Martin had the moment to himself and must have seen her since he appeared to be telling the drifter what had to be said. She couldn't get to them in time.

"THEM LAWSONS MOVED in twelve year ago. Just them two. Died in that damn fire maybe ten years. That there foundation's 'bout the only sign folks had lived there. Weren't no kin around so Irene and me we bought the hay field and now the rest of that land, it's gone to hell. Got that mesquite and juniper movin' in...damned useless.

He wanted to sit down again. More information than he could use. Made no sense to him. In all the years walking and taking sick and scared half the time, then freed from worries by what was bound to happen, he'd come back around to his own

6

childhood and didn't know where he was because the old man had moved.

Even though he'd been born fifty miles from here, he'd grew up some to a stunted eighteen, found who he was and never stopped moving, fearful of what was going to catch him.

Before the woman came roaring up, he answered a question the old man never asked. "Been called Mack since I growed. Just want to let you know."

Then he had to ask; "How'd you know...'bout the Lawsons. I never...said the name." The old man grinned, loving the moment; "'Member how your pa looked. Mack. You got that same long face, bones from a picture your pa showed of your real ma." The boy showed his surprise; Martin grinned, enjoying a long-held memory. "Knew your ma before she left, you got her eyes too. Knew them both to the County court house when we had that trial."

Touchy subject Martin knew, too late. Woman had left her babies, living and dead, and her man and no one heard from her again. He tried again; "Your pa remarried after...you was gone. She was a decent woman."

The boy showed nothing to his face, only tired, maybe hungry, but there was no reaction to speaking about his ma or the past of his separate family.

Irene broke in between the two men, paying her husband little mind. "You come up to the house, child. I remembers you.

Don't pay Martin no mind, come up and I'll feed you. Looks like that ain't been done often enough."

Martin thought later, as he leaned forward to shuck off socks that had a hole in then and finally peeled himself free of the sweaty bib overalls, that it should have been him to make the offer, that as the head of their meager house, Martin could have shared what they offered with a boy too damn weak to do more than say 'yes'm' and follow his wife into the sparse kitchen and sit on a bench, watching Irene as she put together a meal 'though weren't but a half hour past two..

MACK SLEPT IN the back room; there were clean sheets, the bed didn't sag much and there were no fleas. Irene wanted to wake him next morning, boy'd slept more'n fourteen hours and there were chores always needing to be done. Martin said let the boy sleep.

Irene almost ruined the home-coming by wanting to call the boy, the drifter, the sad man aging beyond his years, she wanted to call him 'Henry' like she remembered from when he was a boy.

Martin stood firm, unusual for him but this time Irene was wrong.

The name was Mack, not a given name by saddened parents but a grown name, 'Mack', as if the name Henry Lawson would be forgotten and folks would know the tired man only as Mack.

This once, Irene was wrong and Martin was determined to let her know. Mack it was, period.

ABRUPT

two

No matter how I think or consider or plan, a better nature takes over and the words come out first person. Me, I, no one else, so I (that's me) will go with what presents itself.

At the very end I understood what had been the basis of my life, and yet I found little peace or acceptance. I had lived so long with the knowledge of death that the actuality had me angry and feeling cheated by mere existence.

Too bad life doesn't come in neat and logical chapters.

THE BABY CRIED in endless gasps, cried like its older brothers, who each cried and then were quiet and then, alone and so small, delicate as they were ill, could not digest mother's milk or any of the concoctions made by a mother's helper, a nurse. As a last hope, a doctor came in and very carefully went over each child, distanced by birth from each other by at least several years, each baby pale and limp as it got older.

Various formulas were tried and then, sadly and with no trumpets or exhausted acceptance, one by one the babies died. First, the oldest-born died alone, quiet, all attempts at any kind of life leaving the infant body in a moment when there could be no division between life and death.

The first child died before living a year, and the parents mourned, together in each other's arms, then the man had to return to work and the woman tried to find life in running the big house, keeping it warm by having the young girl bring more coal to the rumbling furnace, and keep water hot on the back of the black cook stove.

There was too much needing to be done for her to grieve; unlike her husband there were no outsiders, no neighbors except housewives and cowhands who lived miles away. And always numberless chores. The Southwest at the end of the 1800s was barren, too distant for women to help each other.

The second child was born in 1896 and he too contracted the illness, coughed and choked and barely lived six months. This time both mother and father did not formally name the child and expected little comfort when the infant succumbed to whatever it was that killed babies with no access to hospitals and medicines.

Neither parent thought that anything could have saved their child. The mother turned to her church for sustenance, while the father went back to the hard work and focus of running a dried-up, tired, waterless ranch on poor ground.

When the third baby came in 1899, both parents were removed, distanced, concerned that they would be hurt again. There was nothing mean or cruel about either of them; they only sought solitary protection from the inevitable. Any attempts at a disinterested and casual intimacy had been urgent and infrequent, based instinctively on the knowledge that their combined genetics created an unbalance in the resulting child. But at the moment of conception, the primal urge had taken over common sense. Against better judgment, another child was born.

At the age of three months, this third child cried endlessly, would not nurse and consequently did not gain the expected weight, nor reach any appreciable growth.

At four months the child had a high fever and a rattle in underdeveloped lungs and the local doctor only shook his head and looked down as he told the parents that this infant, like the other two, would most likely die in the next month. There was nothing to be done.

Two days later the husband came in for supper, expecting a set table and food cooking on the stove that allowed the kitchen, the entire house, to carry that smell which meant home and comfort and some small rest from the demands of trying to live. An invitation to try and enjoy the present life despite the inconvenient sadness of losing two children. Three, now that the latest infant was showing the inevitable signs.

The house was cold, smalls gasps of an exhausted child came from the back room, near to the warmth of a stove, if there had been any intake of fuel.

The room was cold, the stove a lump of unheated metal. When the husband went to investigate the sound, there was an infant, crying in dry gulps, face and mouths covered with mucus, a soggy, filled diaper the only bit of clothing on the child's thin body.

Father and son were alone in a cold house; no food, no warmth, no subdued voice calling out to whoever was there.

They never saw the mother again; no one in town knew where she'd gone, there were a few dresses missing, some unmentionables pulled out of a bureau. One suitcase had been used, just one suitcase to hold the contents of her life.

Despite all considerations, the infant survived. The father hired a series of farm girls to keep the house livable and feed the child, when they remembered.

The boy grew in abject and deliberate neglect, never caring much what his father thought or did, hearing stories about his mother and slowly realizing he was less than interested. Women, the older big-busted females filled with a woman's driving instinct, tried to smother him, which he found amusing as he understood the words, for in their own way the simplest pun put in context how the world saw him. A small child being pulled to an interchangeable ample breast. The unmentioned symbol of a missing parent.

It was not how he saw himself. Having no mother and a distant father allowed him all the time in his world to wander and learn with little supervision. He already knew more than his father could teach him.

Three days after he first went to school

a note came home from the school administration, demanding that the boy have a
name. He was six, a slow starter as he was
small for his age, and he needed to have his
own name. He'd been signed up as 'Baby'
Lawson. There had been a name, bestowed
on the first baby, dead before its first year.
The wife tried again; this second baby was
bravely name; Henry Miles Lawson. The baby
died and was buried next to its brother.

His father thought on the matter as
this month's serving girl served up dried
potato salad and reheated moldy beef hash.
He decided that, despite the wife leaving, the
child growing into no name, the family line
would try again.

The boy's first name would of course be
Henry, after his grandma's papa, middle
name Miles after himself, the boy's pa, last
name of Lawson. There, down on paper it
looked, well, quite proper and ordinary.

The boy went to school with a name on
a grimy piece of paper: Henry Miles Lawson,
and for the years he spent in school, no one
ever called him anything but Henry. He
wasn't worth a nickname for no one cared
enough to bother with such a small and
useless child.

And in the beginning, until he was
ready for the seventh grade, no one except a
few forward-thinking teachers thought much
of the boy beyond an abstract pity. Of course
he was slow, under-developed, a weakling
damaged by his unwanted birth and the early

desertion of his mother. That his pa didn't think much of his son was too obvious to be mentioned.

The boy, Henry, knew almost nothing about his family or the tragic past. No one told him there were two other boys in the local cemetery, both with the same last name, babies who never saw the fullness of their first year.

Inside, where his private world existed, Henry watched, observed, and understood what was meant to be denied. He was to be afraid, weak, a source of social pity without the generosity of what could be possible.

Halfway through the eighth grade, his pa took him from school. Needed a hand on the farm, the old man said, took the boy with no notice to the administration and that was the end of any formal education.

three

I had no idea and no I'm not asking for sympathy or using ignorance as an excuse; my father had said little as I grew up and I don't know if he was ignorant or thought the facts had no value.

Working for my father from when I was almost fourteen, few people took notice of me. I was a boy, not much to look at; small and shy, I preferred the background, let my father hold court, have men listen to him, for then they paid little attention to me.

If my pa worked me too hard, or pushed on hours and chores, I would run out of breath; Pa would pound my back and curse me until I could almost breathe and he would look past me, shake his head and we'd go back to work. I hated those hopeless moments.

Puberty came inside me rather late but I had no idea, no one to tell me. The changes in my body could have been a surprise except for my watching the farm animals. While I lacked much of a proscribed and predictable education, by observation and a certain amount of shock, I began to understand how a male like me could turn into the form my father presented. Strength, breadth of shoulders, a deeper voice and that beard that on my father was rough while on my face the growth of hair was slight at first even as it was new and out of place.

When I turned eighteen, I went to the draft board in the town nearest our ranch and they were glad to have one more recruit to fight the European war, until the docs got hold of me and shook their heads, collectively and alone, at each test.

I did not pass, hell I didn't even make the 'stay home sonny' group. What I got by way of explanation opened a lifetime to me and scared me at the same time. And explained everything when I had time later to think on things.

My lungs were nothing but scar tissue and rot, one of the docs said. The heart was enlarged, pushed to the limit trying to pump oxygen through mush. One doc said what he felt was the truth and those others, they kept nodding their heads as they were unwilling to spell out the truth.

"Go home", the doc said. "Make peace with what you have and be careful, take the rest of your life real easy...." As if he knew something I could never understand. "Not your fault, boy, the damage was done long time ago by a different hand."

It was my life and some unknown doc was telling me how to live it. First thing I did when I got home was to storm out and grab my pa, hold him close under the jaw with his filthy shirt, and yell at him. Now that I can stand back and consider so much of life, the picture of scrawny me, a mere eighteen and no bigger than a miserable calf in late winter, grabbing that hard-muscled rancher, yelling at him, I can almost smile at the absurdity. And that unremembered doc's concern at how soon I would die, well that man too was wrong. It took me more'n ten years to match his warning. Death would come early, but not for a while and these years I would live as I chose, knowing instinctively that little would come back to haunt me.

ON HIS SLOWED return from the Army Recruiter, Henry Lawson worked through what he'd learned, remembering back to an unsettled childhood and an odd growing up when his papa pulled him from middle school.

Kind-hearted and unimaginative folks kept telling Henry how his mother had chosen a godless life and now Henry could accept the church and rest in the safety and love of the entire congregation.

He had time to think, for he'd chosen to walk instead of taking the bus and looking out the window. He needed the time to understand. Too much, too big a burden; he looked at dying, knowing what it meant even as he could not add the knowledge to his few years with so much time waiting ahead of him.

With the stop-and-start distance towards home, a lot of his past life made sense. Indeterminate old ladies with kitchen-widened hips and a tightly-strapped bosom had offered up their brand of religion as comfort to the motherless boy. Once he had a greater understanding of language, their supposed sympathy underlined his loss; a disappeared mother, a father who was present but rarely talked to his son.

The so-named Henry Miles Lawson was refused first by indifferent silence and then a vocal rejection to escape all attempts by these endless women, and the few men who cared, to lessen any break in the boy's sense of worth.

WALKING BECAME A balm for Mack. This was now his chosen name. He would no longer accept the title given by his father. He was Mack and he could pick a direction of his own, safe that unless he spoke of a future destruction, no one could look at him and know what deadly seeds had been planted as the infant was formed with his parents' flaw.

Soon enough, Mack learned that the simple act of walking strengthened ligaments and muscles unused for most of his short life, and challenged the weakened heart.

If he took short rests, found enough to eat, then he could move on forever and no one needed to know. He scared himself with a list he might never experience. Looking down at his feet he was frightened even as he walked, foot rocking on the heel, opposing foot lifted to bring him forward. Natural, simple and holding his inevitable death.

His mind went quickly to the impossible: running, even to the corner to buy a paper, racing a horse, chopping wood. And he would not consider the more intimate dimensions of life; a woman, a simple kiss. Sex.

Walking, it seemed, gave Mack time to think of what definitely lay ahead and he could not plan or prepare. All the threads of any life, marking paths that a man could or could not take, meant no difference in the end; for him it would be endless silence no matter what he did until then. Sooner or later, Mack would run out of threads.

Seeing the familiar house from a distance stirred Mack, bringing a furious, buried anger to the surface, leaving a young man for once at the mercy of unexpected emotion.

THE DEPTH OF the boy's fury surprised Miles. He would laugh except that the occasional fist hit a soft spot and Miles spent too much time prying the fighting arms loose while he tried to explain to the boy about, oh hell he'd have to slap the child until he quit. Then maybe Miles could explain.

Miles Lawson caught one of the fists, pulled the arm up and around until the boy stopped fighting and there was quiet. Even the damn-fool team of horses had quit chewing on the late hay to placidly watch the free-for-all.

Now Miles could see the boy's face and for a brief moment he felt a rare pity. The boy's mother was in those pale eyes, fury etched his face, telling the old man what the child would come to look like; his ma, angry at the old man. Always angry.

Wasn't the boy's fault, he guessed, boy wasn't old enough to chase his ma off the ranch. Just bad luck, Miles reasoned, then he took a cold and distant look; the boy's face was white, too thin, body perfect for a field scarecrow, and knew he'd been wrong.

For that one moment, Miles studied his son. That he should have done this years before came to mind. The boy was thin, yeah, nothing unusual there. But there was a surprising strength to the lean body. That illness, well it hadn't changed the boy much. Maybe it was inattention but Miles saw the boyish face, the dirty hair too long over the eyes and down the neck. Woman's hair, the boy's ma come out in the surface; same pale gray eyes Miles had once upon a time been captivated by. Now he almost hated the boy's look.

Hadn't been prepared though for the strength hidden in that wiry frame. He'd been accepting what other folks thought of young Henry without taking a good look at the boy hisself.

He tried; "Son. Henry!" Guess that harsh voice still had a ring to it. The boy stopped fighting. "Ah hell boy, put some blood to you and you look just like your ma. Couldn't keep flesh to her neither." It was more than he'd ever said to the boy about the woman left them all those years ago. Must be something to the kid after all. Even pale and underfed, the boy took after the long-gone woman. Darker skin, from the woman's family Miles hadn't cared about, tough even though the boy could hardly stand. Damn slanted eyes looking hard through their damned sky-light color.

Guess he'd have to do some telling. Boy deserved something, now the U.S. Army had done its worst. "You was born poorly. Need to tell you, there was two before you didn't make it. Buried them over by the cottonwood, thought I'd start a family graveyard. Not much sense now, only you and me left."

Miles thought about the woman and knew he couldn't say those words, too close still, an old wound never healed.

Finally Miles Lawson took a close look at the underfed and furious result of two people who at the moment of conception had hated each other for what they produced, and that look left Miles with an unsettled shame. He perhaps owed this boy some kind of a life.

"Henry...ah." Miles found it impossible to continue. "Boy, you got born and your ma, well, she left. Can't blame her." He wanted to add, 'it weren't your fault,' but he couldn't

Miles felt tears blur his vision while the boy twisted in his hands. There was something owed to the child even as he became a man. Time had not given the old man access to the right words. Henry had grown despite being told he was worthless, by the town and school, by those in his classes and now by the U.S. Army, which might as well be the whole damned country.

four

It never had felt right to me, something inside was wrong that no one told me until my father fought back and then I understood. My own father could pick me up and throw me around, even though I was eighteen and supposedly a man, a much younger man.

Growing up I knew, a reality in front of me that said everything physical was not what it was meant to be. Things did mix; Pa alone was broad-bellied and squat, faded in the blue eyes, hair holding enough color to tell you it once grew from his scalp in a deep black color. Strength, in the rough hands, thick arms, those damned bowed legs that gave him a rolling gait 'though he'd never left me long enough to go to sea.

Look in a mirror, a stilled pond, the shiny hood of a new car we never bought, and there it was, the opposite of my pa shining back at me so I didn't need to ask. I had to know the other half of me was from a woman what would be called my mother even though I never saw her or her likeness, except as I grew and recognized the side of me that wasn't Pa.

Even though the truth had been hidden, always a word or thought I didn't understand but felt, something; even though I went through childhood unharmed physically while conscious that such behavior wasn't right, what my father told me at first made no sense.

ABRUPT

Something was wrong, something terrible early–on made life a gamble.

One thing everyone learns whether they want to or not is that we all die. Eventually. What makes this truth bearable is knowing it comes at the end of life except by accident, which none of us knew to expect.

Expect for me, once I was told and understood. It would happen and I wouldn't know until that final moment when it was done.

We all accept risks, we all know a central truth. From what Pa said, however, I was born made certain that death walked with me, not waiting, not an accidental result but a death lurking inside me, greedy to be my sudden end.

The only fact to be made clear was the Army's refusal when healthy and even not-so-perfect young men were needed, desperately, as the United States entered the European war and I was turned away, not good enough. Flawed. Now it was a choice, to embrace what I had or to whine and quit.

I stepped back from Pa's holding embrace, suddenly, completely, freed from his conceit that I was a sorry substitute for a natural son and was instead an imposter, a distant child carrying an abbreviated life sentence.

I LEARNED MY sentence from a tired, deflated old man sitting on a thick-seated chair as he quietly explained the closed past to me. He used words I wanted to block out of my world but he kept talking, eyes averted, a big hand occasionally brought to cover his face as if he didn't want to see what words could do.

It is easier now, when the weight of life has been dropped and I can relax, that the words back then drew an ugly picture which I was unable to escape.

"YOUR MOTHER AND I we had a son which was everything to us. Made us a family." The old man wiped his eyes again. "Complete, we was. A family."

Had to give it to him, the old man tried, even when there wasn't hope, or any possible answer. I shook my head, whatever had happened, this man and I were never a family.

"HE DIED. THE baby." Too much for the old man, who squeezed out a tear, quickly wiped it gone. 'We went on, your ma and me. Couple years later your ma was pregnant. We went to a doc, got a list of goods and limits on what she could do." Another hesitation where nothing could be said to dissolve the truth.

"This one too, he died. Boy again, lived almost a year then he was gone. Shook your ma something terrible. We never talked but we stayed apart, you know. Not like man and wife, but we worked the place and never spoke on it."

He stopped there, Miles Lawson, without the willingness to continue. His boy, their son, sat removed from Miles, his face bland, as if the telling that branded his pa meant nothing to the child. All these years and Miles in his heart blamed the boy for the woman's desertion.

That the baby, grown up now despite all predictions, looked like his ma, dark-blond hair and the lean build, that skin and color; only the eyes belonged to the boy alone. Miles Senior hated those eyes, they looked straight at life and defied what had been a promise at birth. Damn those eyes, and the knowing hidden behind them.

What came next was hurtful to say out loud; Miles had never said the words, not even to himself in those first empty weeks. "Then she was pregnant again, we'd stayed from each other, fear I 'spect. Still we were married and...."

Words that could not be said to the boy, a result of one man with one woman. The boy had to know, he'd shown himself too damn smart to not know.

"The baby came on time. Sweet little boy...you know." A deep breath. "You."

His old man's lips caught on ragged teeth and Miles coughed around his filthy hand. Words had to be said.

"'Bout six months in you got something, no one ever named it but you turned quiet and poorly, not eating, just nothing. Them damned eyes of yours they looked at me and your ma, coughing even as you tried to tell us."

Air left the old man; words hurt in his throat. How could the rest be said.

"Came home one night, tired, wanting a meal and some comfort from my wife." He stopped, coughed; "She was gone, you was done waiting, lying there hot and sticky in a wet diaper. No food, nothing in the wood stove. Nothing left."

Again, too much to say. "Doc told me you was...well I knew what to expect. Hired me a girl when I could, looked for my...your ma. Then it was a year, two, three and four went by and I saw you was alive, puny yeah, and slow. So I thought."

THERE IT WAS, laid out. 'My ma.' Not really a question. "Never saw her. Again. Was some reports but...." It was all the old man had and he couldn't look at the boy. Their boy; his boy.

Henry Miles Lawson stood very slowly, touched his father briefly on the shoulder, feeling solid bone and only the slightest quiver of tightened muscle. He knew, no words or sideways looks. But he knew.

It took perhaps ten minutes to pack. So little was important, there were no toys or symbols of a childish past. First there was a hidden stack of money, saved religiously over the years, mostly from small amounts at Christmas and his spring birthday. None from his pa, who doled out pennies perhaps on rare occasions, and never to his sickly offspring, where its gift would be pointless.

ABRUPT

Mack took only a few clothes for not much would fit him or last more than a month or two. No one could claim that the father ever spent much on family comfort.

He took a blanket to sleep in, a warm jacket seen better days. Two pairs of faded jeans, shirts he wore most days, an almost-new pair of canvas shoes, and a pair of hard-worn work boots would do for a while.

Not much for a short life. Mack found he didn't care. For one moment he looked up to see his pa staring at him. Mack half-smiled, knew he wouldn't tell the man the new name Mack was using. No point, the old man sure wouldn't care or ever need to use it.

Mack hefted the rolled blanket with its few possession held tight, set the item from his left shoulder to rest on his right hip, as he'd seen done by other nameless men moving around the country.

He had to start somewhere, learn from those who lived a life put on him with no prior knowledge or sayso. Was early spring now, gave him time to work, to pick up what he needed to survive before that cold winter made living a misery. Until next early spring.

"Pa, thanks...I guess." Mack hesitated, the old man made no gesture to keep his son at home.

"So long."

Two words that came from father and son, mumbled, said and not meant to be heard.

five

I was eighteen, legally a man, schooled only to do what I was told. Each step took me closer to a place I did not know or recognize and found to my surprise I did not care. A world I never conceived opened for me. Traveling with me as a shadow was what the Amy docs told me. I was unfit. Unfit for duty, not good enough for cannon fodder. Rejected as useless.

It was for me to come to terms with what I learned or was told.

THE FIRST STEPS felt like freedom, until Mack realized he had no direction, no orders or indications, no 'back forty' to harrow or a filthy pen to shovel out and add sand for a firm base.

Nothing. So he walked, slow and deliberate, wanting to check out the speed he could maintain. That simple task of checking movement against the rise and fall of his heart could determine the rest of his life.

To hell with it; Mack made a quick survey of what little he knew and decided he would not let what the outside told him direct his life. He'd missed so much, now he would find out on his own what lay ahead.

THREE MILES PAST the village post office and general store, Mack stopped, leaned over and tried to breath. Wanting to holler and shake, get someone's help went to war inside him; Mack knew, he focused on drawing air, filtering it out through clogged lungs – no he would not give in to the panic riding him. Only a few miles, damnit. No one ran away and then quit after a few miles.

He stood, gingerly, letting the short breaths strengthen his heart, slowly work towards a more normal rhythm.

Then he walked on with moderate steps, recognizing speed and exhaustion would become his enemies if he pushed himself. Or even walked as those around him did, with no restrictions or concerns.

His first steps on his own, and Mack was intent on taking a few more steps, a break to calm his breathing. Not look back. Walk until he disappeared.

IT TOOK THE old man maybe five hours, when it was getting towards dark and boy was no place to be seen, to realize the boy had actually gone. Damn it he was hungry and the boy was almost a decent cook if the taste of food meant much.

No sign of the kid. Miles had watched the boy pack his few belongings and they never said much to each other, just Miles watching while the boy rolled and jammed and folded until all items flattened and fitted into each other and disappeared into the shape of a roll that fitted itself across the boy's back.

Miles had shrugged as he watched the boy disappear at a maddeningly-slow pace; hell it would hours at that walk just to make town with any dignity intact. And no matter, the boy would be back when evening came. He would be shamed and hungry, without a chance for food.

Now, the house turned blank, no lights and no smells of something burning or undercooked. Not even the decedent sound of pots clattering, a fire putting out even heat.

A YOUNG WOMAN watched with indifferent curiosity as a traveler passed from the side road next to her house, to stand a long moment staring at the few cars on Main Street. Town wasn't much, maybe two blocks of simple homes, a general store filled with what a rancher might need, no stop lights or signs as folks knew each other and strangers rarely passed through.

A man on foot, now that was different. Anna, she was meant to be watching the young ones, for it was almost supper and their ma hated cooking in crowded and noisy kitchen. Little ones, though, four of them come to life one right after the other; they sat in the yard to the edge of the back step and waited, dirt ringed on their mouths, hands taking hold of more dirt. Only food kept them quiet, knowing Ma would take a fit iffen they tried for inside.

Annie her pa called her, she was the oldest by eight years, going on fifteen now and probably more curious than she need be but no one was stepping up to tell her where she was. Her body changed, filled out and she'd grown hair in places no one told her would happen.

ABRUPT

No one would answer her question. No thought to how she felt. The babies were crowded silently around the back door. Annie went to the front yard, letting the half-rotted fence be her barrier from the strange man.

"You, where you from?" Starting a talk was unfamiliar; her family shushed her when she wanted to share something. No one ever listened.

This one stopped and looked at her. She couldn't see much of his face, had him a collar pulled high, an old hat jammed on sideways but she figured he was light-haired which meant maybe light eyes. A kid but older, why the hell hadn't he gone and joined up to the Army like her two hard-tempered brothers.

Just a kid. "You headin' someplace?" The boy shook his head, wiped a hand over his mouth; "No, ma'am." He took a gulp of air. "Just goin'."

Annie scratched at her head. Odd answer. "What'd you mean?" He panted some, seemed tired but not willing to stop. Annie put up a hand and he came to her as she heard Ma yelling to the little ones, 'come in to eat you'all.'

"Mister, you follow me. Looks like you need feedin'. I'll tell Ma 'bout you." She ran toward the back door, motioning for the boy to join her. He moved slow, as if doubts walked with him. Annie grinned to herself even before she told Ma. It was fun having a man to herself, nevermind Pa always said she was too young to date but old enough to take care of the youngsters. Annie didn't think that was fair.

"Ma he's comin' in just a minute. Ma!"

ONLY BECAUSE HE was hungry. Slept in an abandoned pasture last night, thought of trying grass which had him smiling as he studied the dried-out stalks and finally curled up to sleep hungry.

Even as he entered the over-heated kitchen, Mack smiled to himself. No sign of his papa, no one to tell him whatever. Nothin'.

"You got a name, boy? Where you come from, there ain't no buses up here." And there it was, now the world was telling him. Mack half-laughed to himself as he pulled his filthy hat off, resisted wanting to run a hand through his mussed hair all the time not looking at the girl.

How'd he end up here and why would he care since that pretty child was offering him a platter of steaming meat and what looked like sliced tomatoes and something bitter that had to be turnip.

'Mind your manners, boy.' A vague memory reminded him and it sure wasn't his papa's voice. "Ma'am, name's Mack. Mighty kind of you, all this."

The mother looked at him oddly as she pulled the youngest child into her lap. "S'alright boy, you eat now." That was the end of any talk. Mack, the unnamed mother and the girl, and those babies, they turned to the food and yanked, and pulled until all those mouths went to work and attention was no longer on Mack.

He ate slowly, between short breaths, almost dizzy with intense hunger even as his belly hurt. Sharing with strangers removed Mack from reality. Silence filled with mouth-sounds, the babies gurgling to move strained food into manageable lumps. Wide grins intended to appease Mack left rings of food around each child's lips. There were four close in age, and the girl.

He glanced up and found he was being watched. Annie, that was her name; limp brown hair hung in thick ringlets, her eyes were dark brown and narrowed, as if what she witnessed did not please her. When Annie realized that Mack was studying her, she patted her twisted hair and her mouth, brown with meat juice, moved into an odd smile.

"G'on boy, eat your fill. Won't be no man come home tonight. Gabe...my pa he's been took by the Army. Wonderin' though how come you don't join up." Her words were mild, commonplace in these war times but the wound dug into Mack.

He could barely expel the words, a confusion of the past and the present dismissal by a distant Army. "Tried, ma'am. Got turned away for health reasons." All he could think of to say. He would not tell the world of his weakness. This was his first time having to explain, knowing the question would be asked too often.

WITH MA DEMANDING the man's attention, Annie could stare much as she wanted. Their supper guest wasn't much at first glance, kind of skinny to her taste but his eyes were not what she expected. Sort of a hardened gray she couldn't name but liked the odd spark as the man struggled to find an answer.

Ma didn't seem to care what the boy's words told her. Indifferent to most things, excepting maybe Pa's occasional touch where they both laughed and Annie couldn't seem to understand what they found so pleasing.

Now the boy had the grown-out end of that haircut common folk found pleasing; a neat passel of hair on top, sides clipped close to make the man under the cut look more like an indifferent and weak tree sapling. It was what the ordinary man liked, not the old-fashioned bushy sideburns and fancy beards of the past years.

This boy had once sported the popular shearing but now his hair, a mix of pale yellow and streaks of gray, was thick and almost curling at the neck. Odd, she thought, and kind of cute. Certainly not what most of the school boys wore; sheared by their pa when he found the time.

Skinny, not much to look at yet Annie was intrigued. She'd not bothered to study the boys as school. The older ones, more interesting, were mostly gone to the war. Even her pa had joined up and left Ma and the passel of kids, and Annie having to listen to her ma with few answers about growing up.

This stranger, who seemed different in looks and well, how he thought, was a new species that Annie wanted to explore. "Ma, gimme a slice of that meat." Her ma passed a plate, the 'guest' pulled back, hands high, the plate before him empty yet he did not ask for seconds. In fact, he stared at Annie as if she was cruel. Or at least wrong.

six

Eyes give us away. Not in small moments but the times where our soul is hurt and we don't want the world to know. It's then we are deceived by a look, lids shuttered against any invasion. My first experience was with Annie and her muddied brown eyes staring at me as if she knew the reality inside.

I had to turn away and met her mother's gaze, nothing fearful there, only mild curiosity as if I'd suddenly appeared and she was wondering where I'd come from. Then the youngest child, Sweetheart, almost three, pulled at her ma's dress front and demanded a different nourishment.

MA LET HIM sleep in the barn. Said it wasn't right to have a single man sleep in the house with no husband to keep watch but she couldn't bear the thought of even a bum sleeping outside.

Head resting on his hands, body finally calm as his weight found comfort in the heaped straw, Mack watched the outside town turn off lights, ready for sleep. Sleep was impossible for him; his eyes burned from no sleep, and he found himself panting.

She stood above him; Mack first noticed her worn socks above scarred brown boots. Her legs were a lighter brown, scratched and bitten, a thin cover of faint hair as if she were playing at an older girl.

Finally he realized he must have been sleeping for he hadn't heard or seen her approach.

She sat down and back on her heels, her red check skirt pulled too high so that in the near dark, the harsh white band of cotton between her legs was startling. Meant to preserve her modesty, the glistening white disturbed him. In silence, no words needed, Mack received the invitation. Sensations moved in him between desire and the conviction that the child had no idea what she was offering.

Here it was, a part of life denied him, good ole Henry Miles Lawson. His papa never talked about sex, told his son the animals would teach him. Don't go bothering his pa with damned fool question.

Turned out there was no need for the discussion and Mack found breathing even harder. More for him to accept and damnit.

"What's wrong, ain't I pretty enough?"

HE WASN'T MUCH, kinda scrawny and dressed in near rags, old farm clothes, boots 'bout wore through but the eyes showed kindness, the manner was gentle and Annie wasn't used to concern and even that he made her laugh.

She did what she knew, from watching her folks; she reached her hand out to touch his thigh, just above his knee. Not so bony like she thought it would be even as it registered that he gasped, then coughed and shifted on the rustley straw bed.

Her hand went higher as if it didn't belong to her, she watched in a cool removal as if touching a man felt good and it was different, moving her hand up towards where his pants nestled into that fold in his body between his legs. Her parents did this, sometimes laughing, sometimes when they'd been fighting.

"Little girl. Stop." The voice was hard, each breath torn from his chest. She didn't want to stop.

He twisted, turned his body away from her. "Stop."

Tears interrupted her exploration. Now she was shamed. "Annie, you don't know what you're doing." She whined; "I want to know and you're...you're here and you're kind."

"Go 'way, little girl. I ain't neither." He seemed to think, then laughed. "Least I ain't kind, not in this mess."

THEY SAT IN the dark. She moved herself far enough from him she couldn't give in and touch him. He sat up, drew his knees close to his chest and shut himself off from any chance for even polite small talk.

After ten uncomfortable minutes, Annie got up with a struggle, turned herself and pulled at her underpants. As if he had no idea what had been on her mind.

Annie left quietly; when Mack was sure she was gone, he rolled over on his right side, deep into the straw, instinctively wanting to keep any weight off his heart, and as he tried to understand what she had wanted and how he pushed her away, he slipped easily into sleep.

A SMALL VOICE said; "Mister?" Mack studied the simple word. 'Mister?' Had to mean something. Rolled onto his back and felt daylight though his closed eyelids.

No longer a question but a command; Mister!" He smiled even before he sat up and opened his eyes. The voice came closer, sounds wavering but persistent. He opened up, saw a child, watched the chipped white mug held in two hands where a thin beige liquid spilled over the rim.

"Coffee, mister?" One of the children, the oldest he guessed, never introduced last night but not a baby. And not Annie. "Coffee?"

Mack accepted what was left, about half a cup. He remembered to thank the child, who said her name was Renna before she ran from the barn.

Thin all right, a poor mix of coffee water and a skinned tablespoon of watered milk; hot though, and delicious. Coffee all right, couldn't be just water and sure wasn't the chicory mix his pa'd often fed them. Coffee.

Bless the woman. He tipped the cup and drank quickly, finished, wiped his mouth and felt the harsh beginnings of a beard. There was no doubt; his choice to leave home was turning him into a man.

THE HOUSE FILLED with sounds; girls giggling, laughing, yelling at each other. There was Annie, moving with practice through the kitchen, offering porridge and watered milk to the younger girls. She barely looked at him.

The mother noticed Mack; "Boy, here, take an apple and drink 'other cup of that brew. Best hold you for a noon meal on the road." He'd been fed and given marching orders in the same breath. Annie only grinned and gave the youngest girl another spoonful of some grayish liquid.

Mack drank a second cup of the pale coffee-like liquid and put the slightly soft apple in a pocket. "Thank you...ah...both, for feedin' me." Manners, he thought, damn it, manners.

"Thank you, ladies, you've been a life-saver for me and much appreciated."

Time for him to leave, and the only direction he wouldn't take was to the south and west. Everywhere else was his to discover.

"Again, thanks."

ABRUPT

seven

A high-whining truck rolled too close to Mack on a sharp corner and the driver winced, slowed down and waved a hand at Mack, which he took as an invite and grabbed the truck bed, rolled himself into the slats and junk and pushed himself up to the cab back, resting his head on the broken edge of a cracked window.

Took longer to think afterward than to jump, quickly and with little thought. The truck picked up speed, hit a pothole and twisted, threw Mack on his belly, bumped again and Mack was pushed against a side then the tailgate and he cried into his jacket sleeve and was tossed again.

Truck came to a hard stop, Mack kept still as lights flashed and he couldn't tell from which distance and didn't know why.

"You all right, son?" Voice from above, Mack risked opening his eyes. Leafy branches, slices of blue would be the sky, and if he reached out he could run fingers along the rough edge of metal and remember how it hit him.

Then he laughed, briefly, as his ribs hurt and then he coughed. "Son, you get yourself out of the truck. Now." Mack considered the request, then rolled himself, pulled up his feet and then climbed over the truck bed edge.

Standing, feet holding true, able to breathe now, Mack looked at the old man who'd been driving. "Boy, you go 'bout your own way. Don't need a passenger like you, I'm turning here to the feed store, gonna put grain in back. You go on, don't look hurt to me."

There it was, dismissal as if he were no more than a stray cat. Mack grinned; "Yes sir. Thanks for the ride." The truck ride meant a couple of miles he wouldn't have to walk. No need to look back, he was betting the old man had a puzzled look to his wrinkled face.

HE FOUND OUT soon enough that walking hurt; along the muscle pull over the ribs, and there was a new throb in his right wrist, and for all of this he was hungry. Walking to the edge of the small town, a hand-painted sign pointed to a dirt road into brush and mud, and the sign promised 'Abbott' at an unseen end.

Abbott it was, following a narrow dirt road through brush with the occasional abandoned house, a shack maybe with three sides and a wind-torn roof. Still he trudged on, until his chest ached and his pack's weight was unbearable.

A tree half bent, lying against another tree, a thin stream trickling with clear water; heaven to traveling man. He might only be eighteen and not much on size but Mack had decided. He was no bum, or drifter. He had places to go and walking was as good a conveyance as anything he knew. Leastwise he didn't need to feed or shoe a mule or a horse, and the Lord knew there was no gasoline easy to find out here. Walking was the logical choice.

Mack ventured into a rough field, hung his pack off a tree branch, sat on the thick, dried grass, leaned his head on a rough limb and was immediately asleep.

A DAY OFF from school, 'specially in spring, was a true present and Buddy always did the same thing even though he knew there were other ways to spend time.

The horse belonged to his uncle, at least that was what Mama wanted Buddy to call him. Didn't matter, the horse was sore behind until Buddy walked him some. Nothing hard for old Billy which is how the 'uncle' was given the horse. A good home, light work and a way to keep Buddy out of the house for a few hours.

He usually took two sandwiches with him, his favorite being peanut butter and jelly but only if ma had jelly left from a batch she made and sold to a few ladies. Bologna between two slices of bread was a good second. This time Buddy had one of each and he grinned at the thought. Didn't have to make a choice, and he knew where a few old trees offered decent shade while there was grass for Billy to chew on.

Well damn; then he looked around as if his ma could hear him. He said it again; Damn but there was some bum sleeping on that good tree where Buddy wanted to rest and chew on a sandwich and listen as birds and bugs and things hiding in the woods sang to him.

The interloper. Buddy smiled, he'd seen that one in a book his ma took from the library. Son of a...he couldn't say it so he used the polite 'buck' was beginning to wake up. Buddy knew, he'd seen the process with his ma and that damned 'uncle' when Buddy came home too early.

The eyes fluttered then clamped shut, the loose body tightened barely. Buddy watched and this one confused him. "Don't mean to be takin' your spot, boy. Looks to me your bronc knows exactly what comes next." Then the man sighed, coughed and sat up and moving like that, slow and tilted to one side, showed Buddy that something was wrong.

Billy pulled the reins out of Buddy's hand and put his head down to graze. Buddy laughed and heard the bum was laughing too, which seemed to make Buddy laugh harder, as he slid off Billy, remembering to bring the sandwiches with him.

He held up the bag even as he landed on the trampled grass. "You be wanting a sandwich?"

MACK SAT UP through the tightening across his ribs. He studied the younger boy while considering the offer of food and the source of the offering.

Knees of both pant legs badly patched, only one back pocket; both sleeves torn from the grayish tee. Blond hair too long and twisted by the wind, wide blue eyes and a dirty face and filthy hands offering up a treasure. A sandwich, in fact a choice of sandwich.

"Up to you, boy." He watched the kid pull out a wrapped treat. "You take this, it's peanut butter." Here it was, a simple gesture offered by a child. Mack reached out, saw his hand tremble and stopped. The boy's eyes had grown wide.

For that moment Buddy looked straight into Mack. "Here, you take this," and it was a sandwich layered with a thick slap of brown squashed against a deep purple gem-like sauce.

Peanut butter and jelly. Buddy smiled, licked his mouth. "S'good I like bologna" and he took a big bite of the less colorful sandwich, smiled around the pressed meat and bits of bread flaked off.

Mack bowed his head briefly then bit tentatively into the layers, tasting the strong peanut flavor, layered with the grape jelly. Nothing ever could taste that good. He stopped, chewed carefully, swallowed and when he looked up, Buddy was watching him.

"Good, ain't it." Took another bite and the bologna rind hung from his mouth until the flick of a tongue caught the piece and it disappeared.

THEY FINISHED THE sandwiches silently, then Buddy took a metal cup out of the bag and went down to the thin stream, drank as much as he wanted, then filled the cup again and brought it to Mack. The clear water had dirt and a few small rocks floating, and still Mack drank the cup empty.

"Thanks, boy." For all the words and thoughts that could have been said, 'thanks' was enough.

Mack struggled to get up, Buddy put out a hand to help him stand. Mack nodded, Buddy got busy putting a bridle on a now-sleeping Billy and Mack gave the boy a hand up onto the sorrel's back.

They parted quickly, Buddy headed back to the small town, Mack going down a narrow dirt track without looking back.

eight

Few tracks traveled the road. Mack noticed that more often an animal would cross the road at an angle, and there were dusted spots where the animal would have stood and listened.

At first he walked, careful not to scuff the tracks but determined to make a few miles. Ultimately it came to him that nothing rested on his making time, so he would kneel and study what the animals had left for him to read.

There would be scat he could study; some he knew. Coyote scat and an occasional ball of feathers and bone coughed up and dropped by a hawk. Other piles could be raccoon or prairie dog, an occasional dropping from a domestic dog.

Only a few imperfect hoof prints followed the road edge, often intermingled with the split cow print. Mack smiled then, picturing Buddy on his lame cow horse, walking after an escaped steer.

When he finally came through the trees and still on the road, he glanced around and realized there was grass ahead of him, few trees, then the outlines of a chapel, signs of house foundations. The remains of a small village now covered with cow shit and dust.

Mack stood immobilized, head down and panting. Was hard work to get enough air, dizzy, wanting to lie down, unsure he would get up. He braced trembling hands on his thighs and work on drawing in air, releasing it. Hoping.

A loud voice interrupted the struggle. "You got yourself a problem, boy. Much I can do to help?"

Not enough air to respond; Mack's thoughts almost amused him. He did not, could not know what the next moment held. He'd shared sandwiches with a kind-hearted child and now that kindness was about to backfire.

His voice was tentative, close to embarrassed; "There an outhouse nearby?" A loud slap, a coughing laugh; "Well boy you got yourself a real predicament." Laugher turned to real coughing; Mack still leaned over, easier to breath but it limited what he could see.

The necessity of the outhouse was becoming crucial. Mack straightened despite a harsh pull against his ribs. The big-voiced man was horse-back, straddling a stout sorrel gelding big enough to hold the broad-shouldered and pot-bellied man. The man presented a strange source of rescue.

"Boy, you go behind that chapel and there's an outhouse waiting. Watch the setting down, ain't been used much and there might be..." Mack was off, running almost cross-legged, pushed by impending disaster.

WHEN HE WAS EMPTIED, pants safely in place, behind scratched but not bleeding, and his stomach only mildly groaning, nothing to worry on, Mack opened the wood slat door and approached the front of the chapel. His breath was shallow and he knew his heart beat too fast but it was a clear day and he was safe.

The big old man sat on a tree stump; the sorrel gelding was standing close, three stalks of hay hanging from a sagging lip. "You decent now, boy." "Yes sir, sort of." Mack pulled at the seat of his pants. The old man studied him. "Guess you'll do."

"Huh?" "Need me a hand for the upcoming winter. No one here wants the job so I'm givin' it to you."

So much in that statement that Mack didn't like but he couldn't get his mouth closed fast enough to open up again in denial.

"You got a look says you ain't up to hard work and you sure ain't carryin' nothin' to keep you warm so here's a job jumpin' in and takin' care a you."

Man had a way of saying things that almost didn't make sense. Mack laughed and the big man grinned. "What's the job again?" Mack figured whatever came to him was what he'd do.

"So I said, boy. You don't look so good and I'm giving you sanctuary come fall and through the winter to spring and I can't see you objectin' much."

"What's the job is all I'm asking. And yeah I might not look like much but I can do what's needed."

For a moment rage flared between them; not the good humor and unsaid jokes but fury with no basis. Mack gulped air and shook; the big man's mouth went white at the edges. There was a choice, for either or both of them.

"Boy I said you don't look so good but I'll chance you. Got much to say might defend you?"

It was a place Mack had skirted around but no one ever called him on the facts laid out for the world to see, what Mack had not see until earlier this spring. "Mister, the name's Mack." He waited. "Sim Adams. Guess that's me." The two looked at each other, Mack shrugged. "Okay. Adams." The old man smiled; "You're not much on respect are you."

"No. Guess not." "Then tell me what's at you." Mack scratched at his new beard. "Don't guess so." The old man didn't seem to mind. "New, ain't it. You don't know what to see, or think. Bothers you some. Got you to leavin' home. Now, you take that job I'm offerin' and you can spend time tryin' to figure things out. 'Pears to me you're just a kid."

Mack grinned, tight and curious. This had to be what years and experience did for some of the world. Not his pa; Mack shook his head.

He wouldn't tell the truth, only some of it. No one's business but his. "I've been sick and now I need...well I can do the work, just need time to heal." There it was, only part of the truth.

ABRUPT

Sim Adams only smiled "Boy, whatever you say 'long as it's true, well I don't much care. You ain't broke the law, you promise me that. So let me tell you 'bout this winter job."

It was strange and funny, the two of them glaring at each other, a good fifty years in time between them and still Mack felt he was older, more worn down.

"EXPLAIN THIS JOB and I'll see if it's up to my standards." There, Mack thought, go on the offensive first.

"You want to know today's month and day? Might tell you somethin' important." Mack shook his head; he didn't care. "Well I wants a hand I can trust, means keepin' the barn clean, an eye on our private saddle and driving horses."

The older man took a deep breath; "Yeah we got driving horses. Wife and my daughters they want them a fancy new car but I ain't so sure. So we compromise, I keep horses and pay for that damned car and the man I got workin' for me up and quit. He and my women didn't like each other much I guess.

Couldn't be simpler. Mack agreed with a head bob and a hand offered out as agreement. In a few words and a certain willingness, his life was clear for the next few months.

Now he wished to know the month and the day but it was too late. It'd come to him with getting the job started. Then it occurred to him, to ask.

"Why me? You don't know nothing 'bout me and no one nearby will speak to my ethics or the strength of my word. So why?"

The answer came so simple and easy that Mack laughed. "Tried all the boys 'round here and none would take the job. Too lazy I guess. You, you ain't got much ahead of you, not even the clothes to winter in. Figures to me you ain't got much other choice 'cept to die."

Mack had a question; "You're taking on a stranger with nothing to back him. Why?"

Adams rubbed his chin and laughed; "Boy, when I come on you while I was chasing down a miserable steer, you were in distress bad as I've seen. Yet you didn't use no profanity. Real polite asking me what you needed." Adams laughed; "Was funny even as you was in pure misery".

Enough truth in the bald facts as laid out that Mack had to laugh. Never thought manners would be cause for a good laugh.

Sim Adams scratched one ear and sort of grunted. It was a deal could turn out working for both men.

MACK HAD A job and a place to live for the cold months.

ABRUPT

nine

Adams' ranch was to the north of what had been the town of Abbott, past hills bounded by arroyos and a few narrow rivers. Grass went on for miles, which Adams had over the years squared off by miles of barb wire. Mack's job was to care for the horses, which meant three pensioned cow ponies and two pairs of matched trotters.

Adams liked the blaze-faced sorrels, his wife would condescend to ride behind the two blacks, which Adams found to be reminiscent of the horses that pulled a hearse. He didn't like the implication and often accused his wife and daughters of waiting until 'Daddy' succumbed and they could ditch the horses and revel in the new freedom offered by an automobile.

The household was based on an uneasy truce between Adams and his women with Mack in the middle; old Sim might laugh at the joke, but Mack began to understand why the other man quit.

Mack took notice of the few returned veterans, on crutches or set in a wheeled chair, and the distinct lack of young men populating the few local ranches, and even fewer men in the raucous, once-lively town of Abbott, the few times Adams brought Mack with him, always in one of the buckboards with the sorrel team in harness

There was the catch; the wife, married to Sim for forty-eight years, had been content with her ranch life and appreciative of her sturdy husband. And then her oldest child became a young woman. One year of a local college for women sent the girl home for the summer dissatisfied and restless.

Her younger sister, full of bright smiles and an eager belief, sided with her elder sister. Then again she bristled when Aggie talked down to their parents. Now Aggie had the fun of a new hired man; young, awkward around the two girls, the boy was easily teased, about almost anything.

FOR MACK, THESE people, a family of some standing in both Abbott and further west in Trinidad, were an oddity. A past and a future he could not own. The old man was easy and familiar, like so many of the ranchers and farmers in Mack's past. Didn't pay much attention to him, too weak for hard work.

The women, they were different and Mack could almost identify with the girls and women his father had hired. He watched the women gather together and challenge old Adams, he watched them drive a car around the ranch roads but they did not dare drive into town.

Mack shoveled out stalls, repaired fence, brought hay into the barn and worked at any chore the old man needed. He napped both in the morning and again in the afternoon, and stopped frequently to simply breathe. Adams didn't say much. Watched at first, then seemed to accept that while something was different about Mack, it didn't interfere with what needed doing.

ABRUPT

It became a whole new world for Mack; he knew what waited for him, and at the same time all that he had not experienced came together to taunt him. The girls especially; no denying that they were something he didn't understand.

Looking at them, especially when they stood close and couldn't stay still, brought the unfairness of everything. It was twirling hair or breathing deeply, all meant to capture his attention and let his mind, and his body, understand.

What they couldn't know and he'd never tell them was their unintended effect on his tenuous hold on life. For once maybe his pa had been right without knowing, going on instinct and common sense. The girls' appearance, their careless, unbuttoned clothes and bared skin, awoke strange sensations in Mack.

Which could explain why the harsh old man had taken his son from school by the eighth grade and kept him from most temptations offered to growing boys.

Mack picked up another pile of shavings and manure, and threw it into a waiting wheelbarrow. So much for the important items in life. He had a few curiosities and a whole list of what he couldn't do.

Right now he would laugh and strike a pose and let the two girls play words with him. A new sensation he'd missed growing up, now he might as well take the edges and pretend he understood what they were asking.

He had answers; the provocations that create strange sensations in his damaged body came into vivid focus when the girls played for him. He'd seen enough to know the why of that fleeting need, even as he recognized the damage his lungs caused his weakened flesh when sex became a focus.

He damn well couldn't breathe. Heightened sensations throughout his body came close to shutting him down. He wanted to throw a tantrum, stamp his feet and raise fists to the sky and even that amount of efforts was beyond his ability, and that too added to the frustration.

THROUGH THE REST of the fall and into the holidays, Mack was included in the evening meal. Eating with a family that laughed and talked, even argued with each other, was a new and distracting effort. Throughout the meals, Mack was silent, not knowing what could possibly be said, why would anyone disagree with parents?

Mrs. Adams had her say; "Mack, why are you so quiet? Sim's been bragging on how you work hard and can do 'most anythin' and you sit here eatin' mind you, no problem there, but you don't say a word."

She talked while forking the last bite of a well-done roast into her mouth, unaware when bits of chewed meat sprayed those near her at the table.

HE HAD NO answer and wouldn't go into what would provide an understanding. Silence was impersonal safety. Mack could not draw a line where talk was easy, a freedom he'd not ever known.

'Ma'am, my pa talked about work and I listened. That was our table manners." Simple facts, nothing more, no scandal or sly gossip. "Why, Mack, you actually told us something of your life." He looked down, studied the half-sawed slab of meat, the edges of hardened mashed potatoes and could not think of what more to say.

His chest hurt, his face burned; "Ma'am, please...." He couldn't think of the words, the needed apology to free him from the sudden confinement.

"Ma'am, I'm asking to be excused."

ten

The empty bunkhouse was solid, no leaks, no snow blowing through the walls. Nothing like the shack where he'd grown up. So many things from the past were a reminder, the future could be almost anything for Mack, except for the inevitable and unwarranted abbreviation.

He was jerked back to the present from a brief moment of normal human behavior. 'Why Mack, you told us something....' He hadn't wanted to drift into that trap. The bright eyes of both girls, their warm flesh demanded a physical and ordinary reaction. A mother asking, a pa setting back and watching his family. And Mack, who had no answer to whatever these rude intrusive querulous folk who didn't know when enough was too much. They asked without thinking and he was at the mercy of unintended cruelty.

He stood in the middle of the unimaginative bunkhouse, trying to hear what had once lived within the walls. The dirty smell of tired men, sleeping, cursing, all the human responses his life would neglect in its failing attempt to live.

A new sound invaded the empty room, where one single bed held soiled sheets and three layers of blanket. There was a wood stove, barely used on only the coldest night.

It was a girl, the oldest one, looking at him and smiling; "You left us wonderin', you all right? Mack?" Her mouth glistened, she looked sideways at him, then dropped her eyes. 'My god' he thought. 'She's flirtin' with me.' He stepped back, putting more distance between him and what he didn't understand.

All this was new for him, feelings no one talked about, nothing his pa would mention. His body betrayed him, a stirring in his groin, along with a shortening of breath that scared him, even as he felt warmth and a sense of tingling.

All unusual, frightening and made him smile. Looking up at the girl, he watched her eyes widening and then she did something with her body, and her mouth – Mack had no words left to describe how he felt.

He did what was normal to him; he stepped back, felt the weight of the bed behind him and sat down. Head dropped, he fought for enough air.

When he could look up, she had gone. Left him raw, aroused and startled. Gone, no sound, nothing.

In the early morning, Mack left, pointed down the half-frozen road leading from the ranch. Gone to California, he decided, where it was warm. And then this certain girl would not rule his life.

In his sleep he'd exploded; coming awake as his body chose its own way and he'd climaxed, enjoying what surprised him even as he struggled with an unwanted weight on his chest. Disgust, he decided as he woke to sticky wet sheets and a childish humiliation. Shamed in the early day by an act he did not remember.

He left without a good bye or a breakfast, giving up any offer to stay on or a ride to the nearest town.

Walking in the cold air and pale light of a winter morning, the old Henry Miles Lawson, known only to himself as Mack, moved toward a direction he thought would be west. Away from a house, a small, air-tight home with good people where he'd never get to live out his life.

In the clear winter air, a sharp long whistle told Mack a direction and a possible future. He turned more to the left and walked, seeing only grass, distant ridges and an undulating roofline which could be a train in the distance. If nothing else, there was an incentive for Mack, drawing him away from the safety of Sim Adams and his uncomfortable offspring.

THE INTENSE WHISTLE became a slow freight train moving through the few buildings, clattering over the one road crossing, reaching Mack and leaving him with an idea.

It didn't matter where he went as long as it wasn't north – too cold. He hurried, half running at times until his lungs were a reminder. He would stop, gulp air, then walk until he was impelled to run.

The train was ahead of him but it was downhill from where he was and Mack figured he'd push it – run, you idiot, he thought. Don't mind gasps and a band of pain. Run using the sloping hill, run toward the disappearing line of cars, chose an open door, run beside it then grab and belly down, don't mind splinters in the belly. Run.

HE HAD TO roll onto his back, raise his arms and let his lungs struggle, choking him until chilled air worked in and slowly he could breathe.

Then he did laugh; half the pain in his chest was the remains of those splinters tearing at his shirt, spearing his flesh, thorns in his side so to speak but they were on his belly, above his heart, down near his belly button and a few on his left side. Dumb foolish things, and they took his attention from struggling lungs. That particular heaviness was an old friend.

Slowly, moving inches at a time, he backed himself up to a wall, let his body settle, then spent a good half hour picking those damnable splinters free of his chest. Eventually he had a small pile by his right thigh, with only a few dots of blood.

Beneath him Mack could feel the wheels crackle on the track, picking up speed, tearing across the barren grass. Nothing inside the boxcar let him know the particular railroad that carried him. But he did know that ahead somewhere close was a town and more choices for direction.

Rolled onto his right side, Mack curled up with a few shirts as a pillow; he slept, the rhythmic wheels hitting each break in the track, a sound of moving that left Mack with a unconscious grin.

ASLEEP, MACK'S FACE was relaxed; eyes closed, lower lip hanging loose, hands together making a pillow for his head. Asleep he offered up composure to fool any onlooker.

His face was a confusion of age and hard work; he was almost nineteen yet the flesh was close to the bone, from hunger, hard work and genetics. Open, his eyes were light gray, his hair a sunlight mix of blond and gray.

Full on, the face was narrow, a high brow over a once-broken nose and a full mouth. Asleep, freed from worry, the features looked to be of a man in his late twenties; awake and sometimes talking, the boy reverted to his true age.

The clothing was nondescript; a faded plaid work shirt, torn and patched jeans, stained leather boots rotting at the heel. Nothing much to look at, non-threatening while he was asleep.

Long-term illness literally shaped Mack's life and his growth. Lean to thinness, topping out at 5' 9", with the hands and feet of a bigger man. It was through the chest that his body betrayed him. Struggling lungs had given him a sunken chest, tipped posture and a short-breath gasp that occasionally stopped him mid-action.

Then Mack woke up, chest drawing in shallow gasps, eyelids half open so the boy could see where he was before moving. It would hurt an onlooker to watch him sit up, slide backwards until he could lean on the car wall.

The look to Mack's gaze was an instinctive warning. 'Leave me alone', the eyes said. 'Don't come at me.' Then Mack wiped a hand over his mouth, shook his head and tried to smile, even with no one to watch. He knew right where he was; on an unnamed train, traveling nowhere with nothing waiting ahead.

TRAVELING BY TRAIN was passive, no choice, no direction, nothing to do but sit and wait.

For Mack it was a lost time, where he could think about what had ruled his life, what lay ahead of him and how little he could do to alter what waited.

Studying his hands, he could see nothing different about them; callused, veins across the back, broken nails imbedded with dirt. An infected cut across the left wrist to the base of a thumb, hands showing work, evidence of nothing except what tightened his chest and left him panting where another man could take a breath and do what was necessary.

No one looking to Mack for help would get much despite appearances, and Mack hated himself for promising what he could not complete.

The family he'd just escaped were a fine first example and left Mack with less confidence in himself. Guess he'd move on until whatever chased him caught up and smiled as the inevitable meet up against Mack's stubborn hope.

ABRUPT

eleven

Tired of self-pity, Mack scooted to the open boxcar door and stared out. From the look of fences and dirt roads, houses too close together, Mack guessed they were coming to town. The train slowed, Mack saw shapes pulled against each other and he jumped, knew to roll with a shoulder up to his ear, protecting his face as his body met graded dirt and crushed rock.

Flat out, on his belly, hands gripping and kneading dirt, mouth pursed to clear itself of sand and rock, Mack pushed himself to his knees, knowing if he lay quiet, he would stiffen and never move.

Up on his knees, Mack saw the back side of a yearling steer; kicking, bucking in one place, kept from escaping by a length of rope held by a young woman. The source of a continuing dust cloud, obscuring houses and streets, focused Mack's gaze on the rebellious steer and its unwanted confinement.

The woman at the rope's end had the discipline and humor to smile; "Grab the tail and yank, he's going to pull me sideways. Damn it, pull!"

Mack grabbed the tail just as the woman was pulled sideways; she let go, the steer kicked up and back and Mack saw the underside of two hooves too close before he felt his jaw explode, then he fell but would not let go of the tail and was dragged.

LATER, TOWARDS EVENING, Mack woke to a gentle hand washing his face; cool water, soft on his jaw, firm on his forehead. "Thank you, ma'am." He closed his eyes again, jaw hurting and now his chest hurt and he needed to sit up but the woman didn't seem to understand and Mack was scared.

He tried; "Ma'am. I need...." Couldn't find the words or the energy to speak them. He fought to sit against the wall, look her straight in the eyes. "Ma'am...." and realized she was laughing.

"Mister, you took hold of the wrong end of a good Christmas dinner and I bet it's still running. Got my brother and my husband chasing that damned steer with no results yet. But you sure gave us all a good laugh."

"Christmas?"

SHE TOOK A few minutes to tell him; it was Christmas Eve in ten days and the steer was to be slaughtered, dressed out and hung, until cooking time. If caught soon, the steer would be the main course. Dry-aged roast beef, potatoes and all the fixins, even something green, and a puddin' for dessert, made, she said, 'with our Ma's recipe."

The woman's face showed lines around the mouth and eyes, skin tanned except for the white hidden by an ever-present hat. A woman who knew how to work, and who made Mack's inability to hang on to the escaping Christmas dinner a minor inconvenience.

"Ma'am, let me." He took the wet cloth from her hand. "It's not much and my fault." She smiled; "In that case, you're staying here 'till we either catch that damned steer or decide on an old rooster for a good chicken stew. Mister?"

He shrugged; "Mack." And there was a pause, when neither of them responded. She cocked her head. "My name is Mrs. Whittaker...Mack." Said as if the simple name was not enough. He would not help her.

Yet she nodded as if he'd answer a spoken question. "Rhonda." She smiled. "That's my name. My mother read a book." She made the odd statement as if it meant something. To Mack, the reference was pointless; he could read, slowly, and he remembered addition and subtraction and a vague sense of American geography but little else of the few years in school.

THERE WAS SOMETHING biting this man and Rhonda knew enough not to ask. Married to a earth—bound rancher, she smiled at the young man with bruises on his jaw, a lump under his ear, and an affliction she did not yet understand.

"Mack, can you tell me what's wrong?" This simple question seemed to require an extremely difficult answer. He choked, took a deep breath, then another and she could hear congestion and a harsh explosion of air. Then the boy looked straight at her and for a brief moment Rhonda enjoyed looking at her odd helper. Light eyes darkened with unknown pain, ragged hair highlighted by a harsh sun. He was young, face unlined, barely touched except by weather. A kind gaze tinged with exhaustion.

She couldn't hold her gaze; he too seemed uncomfortable and looked to the side. "Mack, what's wrong?" As soft and kind as she could speak, wanting so badly to help.

HERE WAS A choice and Mack had not lived with his sentence long enough to reason out an acceptable and ordinary answer. She offered a chance, but it came from a stranger. Head down, no sense of the woman, Mack breathed quickly, terrified, then he decided. Raised his head and looked straight at the woman. Stringy brown hair, nose peeling from the sun, rough hands burned from their recent conflict. Married, hard-working, yet she wanted to help.

"Ma'am." That was all, he didn't know how to continue. Made him choke as he looked sideways into her eyes and saw only concern; did he read into her look what he wanted to see? Was this a lie; he couldn't tell, didn't know.

His first chance and it was denied; "Ma'am I can't...don't...." He ran out of air and felt his body try to double its effort to breathe, gasping, no room for talk.

One arm helped him sit up, the other touched his jaw where the bruise throbbed.

ABRUPT

MACK LEARNED HE couldn't accept help without caving in to a woman's instinctive kindness tinged with an inevitable sexuality.

It was possible to stand on his own, he could breathe again if he was careful. "Ma'am, seems I'm doin' fine." He thought of the promised dinner running around the grasslands he'd just crossed.

"Mack, you're not telling me the truth. I can see it...." Here she waved her hand across his chest. "It's not just that durned steer hittin' you, it's somethin' else."

"No, ma'am." He could breathe now, almost normal. "I best be going." Anywhere would be better than facing this woman and her generosity.

"Join us for supper, Mack. And spend the night here. I won't argue with you, but...it's almost Christmas."

"No ma'am. Christmas ain't been part of life for me. But I thank you. Won't miss what I don't know." There was no regret or sadness in Mack; he'd known about the holiday through his pa's occasional church-going. "Will stay the night, though, it'd be a pleasure."

She, however, took in his statement as if he was missing a greater part of life. Mack turned sideways before he answered; "Thanks, ma'am."

Rhonda Whittaker shook her head, knowing that the boy's thanks were for more than inviting him for a home-cooked meal and a soft bed.

THE BOY WAS gone before Rhonda and her husband got up to start the coffee and shovel coal to warm up the house.

Mid-morning her husband, Merritt, came inside and poured himself a third cup of coffee. "We caught that steer, Rhonda. So it's roast beef for Christmas dinner. It's too bad...."

Merritt didn't have to finish. She touched her husband on the upper arm; "I know, I wish he'd stayed. It's as if I...." He shook his head; "You tried."

twelve

The result of poor judgment made itself very clear as Mack headed toward what he knew, the railroad yard above town, barren rails laid in pairs, abandoned box cars offering little shelter. And snow, cold wet continuous snow.

He'd left the promise of a bed, warmth, food, and a safety rarely experience. Now he was headed into the snow blasts, coming off mountains to the west, Mack considered admitting defeat and returning to the house he'd just left.

No. Taking short breaths through a stained wrap, part of a stolen scarf wound around his neck; the wool warmed his body, much like the loaf of bread cradled under his coat and a fist full of coffee beans that tantalized him.

Mack never thought of himself as a thief, petty thievery perhaps but taking things that did not belong to him was foreign. But he was desperate.

Still he cradled the bread and contemplated what the coffee would taste like when it was successfully prepared.

A SLOW-MOVING STEAM engine with a line of cars behind it made a cautious trip north, where way up the line lay the grand city of Denver. Three empty cars were positioned between a car stacked with lumber and four cars loaded with wooden crates, hiding whatever was being transported. More cars followed, rattling empty, whipping on the snow-lined track.

Mack jogged a few steps, speeded up and grabbed an open door, pulled himself inside and lay prone, face buried in the wooden floor, inhaling, gasping, chest burning even as he could feel the boxcar tick over joined rails.

Finally he could roll over, the loaf of bread still in his arms, flat now and broken so the aroma became an impossible tease.

Mack chewed on a torn corner of the partial loaf, stopped and rested, then ate another corner and sighed. A struggle followed, where he found himself leaning against the boxcar side, too close to a wide-open door exposing a fast-moving train headed into a growing snow storm.

Self-preservation moved Mack to lean out the door and there, a good distance to the north and west rested a squat dark cabin, tops of poles enclosing what would be a corral. No life, no footprints except for scurrying mice and rabbits.

As he looked and considered where he was going, the long train jerked to a halt, sending the back five cars off the tracks. Forward movement was now impossible.

He couldn't stop; Mack jumped into deep snow and angled himself toward the cabin. As he closed in, the cabin showed no life and few comforts, but there was a tilted chimney and moss-covered logs stacked up near the only door.

Looking back toward the train, Mack saw cars off the track, piled snow at the engine front, and shook his head. That train was going nowhere. For now, at least, he had some place warm waiting for him

Inside, the cabin was rough, chilled by neglect. On further inspection the woodstove and pipe were air tight and with a few rotting logs from the porch, and a handful of shredded newspaper, the small space was slowly warming..

Snow brought inside in a chipped tin bowl soon enough turned to water; meanwhile Mack went hunting out a bent coffee pot and a rusted door stop was strong enough to pound the beans into coffee.

Guessing at proportions and water, soon enough the pot made its noise and Mack waited, figuring he wanted something to stand up to the torn loaf of bread and his own hunger.

Staring around the crude cabin, warmed by the stove, soothed by the pot's insistent noise, Mack knew that behind the simple comforts he'd brought together, there was the matter of his taking what didn't belong to him. For all the needs which brought him to stealing, he couldn't justify what he'd done. It had been his choice to leave; first from his father, then the Adams, now these people, and here he was adapting the abandoned shack to his own needs as if the actual owner meant nothing.

His chest hurt, he leaned against a wall and panted. What he'd done was wrong, still he could not accept what had been done to him, through no one's fault except for not telling him what lay ahead.

ONLY ONE CORNER of the bread was left; cold coffee dregs covered the pot bottom. Mack lay on a grass-stuffed bag, hands crossed behind his head. He'd failed, even with all he'd learned. The stolen loaf was basically a collection of crumbs stuck to a stale crust. And the coffee grounds had no life left to them.

He'd been here a week. The snow was gone, the exposed grass bent and individually frozen. He'd tried a few traps, caught one half-starved rabbit that barely made two thin meals.

Nothing left now. Almost out of the punky, half-rotted wood and nothing but frozen grass and sturdy, hard-dried corral posts. And no ax, not even a knife.

Mack sighed, started to cough and rolled onto his side, coughed harder until he could not catch his breath. Worn out and hungry, Mack shut his eyes, drawn into his private misery.

Nothing left, not even another pot of coffee.

HIS BOSS'D SEEN smoke comin' out of the crooked chimney in that durned shack where the old man froze to death last winter. Rio himself thought maybe the smoke was proof of ghosts, which he'd always wanted to believe in but logic confounded him. Now that smoke'd appeared, well Rio was more than willing to find out for the boss. Wasn't close to spring yet, no mama cows lookin' to birth, so Rio was sent over the dead grass lands to find out who'd taken root in the cabin.

There were thin tracks going away from the cabin, human tracks, probably looking for what might be food. No sign of a horse, and not much wear on the trail. Rio brought his bronc to a halt some distance from the stark cabinet. He called out, got no answer and called again.

Disgust and fear, two distinct considerations, battled inside Rio. He moved his bronc close to the house, dismounted and tied the horse before stepping up on the thin boards to knock on the door.

Rio backed up. A shape appeared near the opened door. An unused and cracked voice startled Rio.

"Yes...yes?" Not much but Rio used the few words to enter the cabin. First it was the smell, of sweat, waste, a heavy scent of disease. Then Rio looked into the eyes of the interloper and he wanted to leave. To go back to his boss and say that no one was there.

The kid in front of him was barely standing, face pale, hands at his sides trembling, even the chest was struggling, rising, falling too quick, as if the boy was afraid and struggling.

"Got some grub to the saddlebags. Some hungry right now, you want to share?" Where that came from, Rio thought. How'd he know what to say. The kid seemed to half-smile, nodded quickly and staggered. Rio himself set the boy down in a near chair before going out to take a deep clear breath, then grab the saddlebags and haul them inside.

The cabin's visitor was asleep, head leaned back on the rocker's slats, hands intertwined on his lap. Rio emptied his bags onto a rough table, back to the too-thin kid who still slept.

He put together two slabs of bread covering a chuck of cold pot roast, thick with jelled gravy and a few slices of potato.

The sleeping visitor woke when Rio touched his shoulder; damn, he thought, as his hand touch bone through a threadbare shirt, this 'un's too damn hungry.

MACK SMELLED FRESH bread and something else. Beef, he decided. More than beef; his mouth filled and he swallowed.

Then he gasped, chest fought to fill and expel. "A moment, that's what it'll take." To ease the savior's concern. When he could open his eyes, the man was standing a few feet back, holding a huge pile of odors and smells that enticed and repelled Mack.

"Tear me a corner...please." That was all Mack could handle. Saving his own life had to be handled with care.

Rio's hands were gentle as he put the bread into the boy's mouth, then cut off a section of beef and smiled into the boy's tight face. "Thanks," was what he got in return.

This close, it was easy to study the upturned face. The skin was pale, even the eyelids showed a pale blue, blue around the mouth. Not good signs, Rio thought. "You want to come back with me? My boss sent me, saw smoke comin' from the chimney. Ain't had no one here since...." Guess the rest of the story wouldn't be what this half-starved drifter wanted to hear.

"Got me a horse we can share. Ranch ain't far from here...." He felt strange tellin' things to an obvious drifter, but this one, his gaze was muddy, hands shakin' and then he pushed himself up to standin' and for a moment, Rio was a might scared.

Then this youngster put the edge of the beef corner into his mouth, chewed some before smiling at Rio. "Whatever you say, I got no set schedule, just don't want to be here 'round Christmas.'

Rio shook his head, Christmas'd come two weeks past. The boy sure was missing time. Looking over the drifter again, Rio decided the thin face and hunched shoulder, and that look to the sunken eyes might have a word or two on the subject of a missed holiday.

THE RIDE BACK wasn't much. The boy hung to the back of the saddle, perched on the bronc's slanted rump and fightin' to stay on board.

Range boss laughed when the spare kid slid off the bronc's rump, causing the horse to kick out and miss, then buck and Rio cursed until he fell off laughing, burying his face in snow and fresh manure. An all-around dustup only it was wet snow and flying hooves.

"Damn it Rio who's the son you brought and why in hell he's so damn thin?" Dick Raynor didn't much hold back. Rio struggled to sit up; the drifter touched his shoulder before moving in close to Raynor.

"Name's Mack. Guess Rio came huntin' me on your orders." Raynor studied his opponent; "You took up roost in a cabin don't belong to you."

Mack grinned, drawing tight skin across his face in the attempt. Bright sun and clear air tightened his chest. This range boss better be quick. "No sign no one was livin' there. I didn't use much 'ceptin' the wood. And it was punky."

For a moment Raynor was quiet, studying the scarecrow in front of him. Damn the kid gave it right back but he sure didn't look like much.

"YOU WANT A job livin' to that shack. Keepin' track of strayed cows, bringin' on some colts come spring?"

ABRUPT

thirteen

He didn't remember much the next month or so, woke up the end of February and Rio told Mack he'd slept, napped, ate, and slept again for six weeks. Mack felt the softness 'round his belly, the weight of a thin beard and long hair around his ears, and said; "Guess so."

The job was there, waiting. Raynor simply nodded and said there was supplies, and firewood, out to the shack. Be more supplies Mack give Rio a list, whenever Mack was ready.

Raynor nodded once, said he'd spoke to the owner, there's be a few doubtful mama cows at the corral next week, Mack needed to be there.

No questions, no where or when, or the more important why. Live in the shack, work the stock and get paid. Simple.

TWO ITEMS OCCURRED to Mack that spring. From the fresh calendar hanging to the outhouse at the main ranch, he was turned nineteen by now.

Mack figured time was recognized by dates. That last fall when it came up, 1918 he reckon, the war in Europe, the one he'd tried to join before learning his life sentence, it was declared done and over on November 11th. Eleven to be remembered; eleventh month, eleven day, eleventh bright and shining morning hour. There would be no way Mack would ever forget the events.

And two years later come spring, having lived and worked out of the old shack, he'd settled in and where he was comfortable, too comfortable, Rio came out to tell Mack that the ranch owner had died and Raynor quit, going to live with a married daughter up to Wyoming.

Rio said all the boys were surprised, no one'd known ole Raynor ever had a wife, or that he was a grandpappy.

Of minor interest was that today was Mack's 21rst birthday. He felt good, hadn't had trouble breathing in a while, and had learned to stay on top of a wild bronc and far enough away from a mama cow just had her calf.

Given a day, to pack and get out after the last pay, with a small bonus, occupied Mack, until he left the cabin behind and realized he had no idea where he was headed. At least this time he had a horse and some honest, useful supplies. Like a fry pan and a coffee pot, with a bean grinder.

A few years in one place; friends, hard work, quiet nights, times when he could get used to reading, even learned to cook as well as ride a bronc. Mack grunted, few skills, not much past a curiosity about what came next.

He'd grown stronger, that much he knew. Maybe he'd moved past what had been promised as a child.

There was a brief moment when Mack laughed at himself; here he was, twenty-one in the 1920s. Laws against drinking were common now, no skin off Mack, he'd never had a drink.

Wore a cotton shirt two sizes too big, faded denim pants tucked into high buckaroo boots. Cowboy wear from a thrift store, and a misplaced pair of knee-length chaps one of the older hands gave him. Most of his outfit came from an earlier time, marking him now as someone different, with outdated skills that warranted only a quick glimpse before any boss would look at another, more modern worker.

Slowly, as he rode the dun, he let a distant time settle in him. Yes he was full-sized now, entered in to the adult's world without excuse or family to support him. With his own history waiting to catch up to him, Mack figured he best look to each day and not worry much on a future. Wasn't the future he wanted, so he'd make an aborted life the best he could.

THE INEXPERIENCED BRONC lifted its feet high over the train tracks going towards another town. Mack sat quiet, silencing himself, giving confidence to the young horse. If he concentrated on what he was doing, only then what might be ahead could dissolve and be gone.

He knew better but there was always hope to keep him going.

MACK LEARNED RIDING lonesome was not in his favor. There was too much time to think, no buddy to ride with him, laugh and talk while Mack listened. All the things he'd missed, working for his pa.

What rode with him now was a silent worry, almost nameless and sinister; Mack shook his head and the half-trained colt jumped sideways and Mack grabbed the horn, hoped no one saw him then realized there weren't no one around.

Well, north was a destination. He'd never been there since he moved into that seductive cabin and had a life, valuable and confining and it seemed to be what Mack needed.

Ahead and to the right was a thin road headed in the same direction so that would become his choice.

A HUGE BLOCK of a mountain rose ahead of him. Bare rock and small cactus seemed to cover the sides, leaving a barren narrow trail pointing to the top.

Wisely Mack rode around the lump rising naked out of the grassland. He saw to the left there were distant mountains, and ahead was a long wall with the suggestion of a road ahead of him; to the right there were canyon entrances and more wall, endless and out of his sight.

He turned the dun colt hard left and the horse decided to rebel. Head snatched from Mack's hand, the bucking display was no surprise and Mack rode it a few strides, then pulled the colt hard to the right, interrupting its course. Front legs tangled, horse and rider sprawled to the ground.

Eyes closed, Mack reached out and felt the colt's ear, rubbed the inside as he thought on what came next.

The voice; "You all right, son?" wasn't what he expected. Having to answer was an intrusion; Mack had to roll to sitting, rub his eyes clear of dirt then quickly put a hand hard to the dun colt's muzzle, keeping the horse down.

"We're...ah I'm...", then he coughed and felt the struggle inside him. "Damn." He didn't mean to swear. Looked up and saw a sad face, a big hand swiped across the mouth, and Mack apologized. It became a struggled; "Sir, I didn't...mean. This was wrong...my fault I guess." He quit then, took his hand off the colt's muzzle and as the animal made a try, Mack stood with the colt, then comforted the horse.

All this time, the sad face belonging to a big hand, the body sitting on a mammoth mule, had nothing to say. Setting that mule like he was in a familiar chair, wearing bib overalls, the mule himself wearing a bridle with blinkers.

Mack wheezed, wanted to sit but thought he'd be better off talking first, keeping the old man from asking. Didn't matter what the old man wanted to know, just keep him from asking. Mack was tired, off-balance from the fall, not wanting ever again to explain.

"Son, you're fightin' a good fight but you can't breathe even if you did nothin' so tell me what's going on." Damn, Mack thought, time's were he couldn't win.

"Just gettin' me back together." The old man smiled, nodded his head. "Go 'head, boy, tell youself a lie but don't think it'll work on me. You catch your breath, climb on that dumb dun colt and follow me. I gots to get on home, chores need to be done."

MACK CLIMBED ON the dun colt as the mule headed west, toward those very distant mountains covered in snow. And it was only when the colt hurried to keep up with the mule that Mack realized the old man was a Negro. Didn't think he'd ever seen one before but he'd read enough during the cold winters, and he vaguely remember his pa talking about such things as slavery and men knowing their place and color of their skin as if were a mark of ignorance or stupidity.

Following the old man on his strong mule left Mack feeling that maybe he was the stupid one, having brought the colt down, and then there was his damned breathing. Stupidity sure could limit a man's life.

"Mister." The mule kept to its long walk, the old man turned his head; "Yes?" "I got lung troubles, had them my whole life." Mack surprised himself; he'd talked out loud, spoke to the truth and guessed he'd come to terms with....

The old man shrugged; "You ain't lived your whole life yet." There it was, said and answered. Mack unexpectedly kicked the dun colt and the horse lurched into the old man's mule which kicked out and Mack had to laugh. Then the wide back seated on that kicking mule started to shake and quiver and a large shout emerged that was the beginning of more laughter. Until the mule and the colt stood nose to nose while the riders wiped runny noses and leaking eyes.

Up this close, Mack saw his companion clearly, for the first time. Ever. The man's cinnamon color of face and hands showed almost no wrinkles or age. Man was younger than Mack had thought, and solid; big hands dark on the backs, the palms light, almost Mack's color. The face had opened into a bright smile, startling white in contrast to the face color. Mack shook his head; he'd never seen before.

Before he could think or consider, he asked; "Where'd you come from?" The dark-skinned man was Mack's first encounter with what was the basis of an odd prejudice. Surprisingly the man answered with a quick smile.

"Now you asked a bunch a questions in those few words. I's got born in Nicodemus over in Kansas. Folks to Nicodemus is all black, a small town you ain't never heard of. Moved myself up here to live myself and no one else."

He seemed to smile then, a quiet, internal pleasure that surprised Mack. "Now I got me a wife and a reason to live each day. She keeps me honest to myself." The smile faded, the dark eyes were intense in their own study.

"What gets you movin', boy? You ain't but a youngster yet here you is. Folks throw you back 'cause you's small in size?" Mack started to protest and the black man only laughed. "Hell, boy, you ain't being insulted, just facts. Me, I had worse said bout who I is, you got a 'pinion 'bout your size is all."

Mack had been told by his pa, knew the word but couldn't remember it. Then the Negro interrupted; "Name is Jacob, my folks took Richardson as their last name. After that damned war."

Slave, that was a fighting word. Mack thought about 'his' war and shook his head. This Jacob was talkin' 'bout his own war, the one freed his folks. "You call me Jacob, here? And you?"

The young man's answer was brief and not questioned; "Mack." Jacob Richardson nodded. "I's goin' home, come along. Letty'll be pleased for the company."

ABRUPT

fourteen

Letty was a surprise, as least as far as Mack's limited experience. There was more to her than her dark-skinned husband. Eyes and skin of a gentle brown, a voice caught in other places, sounds Mack did not understand. Still she welcomed him, overriding his suspicions. If nothing else, he'd learned not to trust those who took him in with little curiosity. More was expected; women, girls, old men wanting a hardworker, or a new son.

He looked for Jacob, who had put away his mule and Mack's foolish dun colt, then came to the small house on a dirt road almost near a thinning town. Mack felt the pressure; "What do you want, Mister Richardson?" Instinct told him to use a formal address, to distant him from these people.

LETTY RECOGNIZED THE stiffness in her Jacob's back and did what she could. "You, Mack, why do you ask such a question?" She knew her voice was strange, often a sound was swallowed, as she had learned from her family, a father from a band of Osage, a mother a captured Mexican.

"Why do you treat him so? Jacob is an honorable man." She could say it no other way. Mack took a back step, refusing to even touch the bottom stair of the small house.

WHAT STOPPED HIM? Mack was a child again, uncertain and shamed by his reluctance, fueled by a long-held hostility from his own pa. Teachings Mack had heard but did not understand. Now he faced the revolution he'd learned in the past few years, up against what he'd been told as a child.

He was no longer that child. Mack took a deep breath, felt a harsh rattle; "Ma'am, mister, I 'pologise for what I've been thinking. Ain't right, I know that." His lower lip threatened to betray him. "I was wrong."

Mack opened his mouth to keep going then he saw what surprised him and put his mind in a different direction. "You've got a truck, Mr. Jacob. I ain't never ridden in one. Least not in the cab." His mind skipped to another peculiar thought; "But you was ridin' a mule."

Letty and Jacob both laughed. Jacob finally calmed enough to answer. "Boy, I drives the truck for work." Then he smiled and it was a glorious thing. "But I rides the mule for my pleasure."

She put a hand on Jacob's arm. "It is not fair to laugh at the boy." Mack blushed and stared at the ground; a woman chose to defend him against her own husband.

"Letty." Jacob swung around; "Boy, you want yourself some honest work?. I do odd jobs 'round town and could use your help. Spring time's busy." As if the man was surprised at his own offer. "You, you can bunk in the barn, ain't no room to the house, but we'll feed you. Part of the deal. Okay?"

"Sure." It was done, sealed with uneven smiles.

THE BARN WAS well-built, no outside light between the tight boards, little air circulating inside the barn. Mack had moved into a warm, enveloping new home. Even the mule, and Mack's own dun gelding were good company. Tied in generous straight stalls, both animals turned their heads and watched as Mack made himself a straw bed, put his few belongings to hang from a wooden pole, the extra shoes close under the bed.

He still wasn't sure where life was pulling him. He'd started by running from home into other folks' lives. No set place for him; those few years living in the shack and working for an unseen boss wasn't much of a life. And now this, what could be seen by others as the bottom; living with a mule and a colt for company, working odd jobs with a colored man as his boss.

Up to Mack himself, he figured. To accept Jacob as a boss, to let the man's wife take care of him; Mack with no last name that he would accept, working for the child of slaves. He shook his head; life had surprises, guess he needed to accept what came to him and do his best.

BETWEEN THE HOUSE and barn there was a shack, snugged up close to the back door but most definitely not connected to either house or barn.

"I could stay there, not bother the horse and mule, or you two in your own house." Jacob laughed. Letty was very gentle; "Come here, boy. Let me show you." Mack followed her, shy from speaking out, and curious. Jacob headed to the barn.

Sides to the shack had spaces between them; the roof was good, no sign of leaks. But inside, there was a different world Mack did not understand or expect.

Plants, weeds his pa would have called them; green things hung from rafters in bunches, soaked in small bottles of different colored liquids. Nothing in front of him that Mack could name.

She grinned; "Herbs, boy. Plants educated folks dismiss as a nuisance, but me, I got taught by my grandmother who learned from her mother. These are healing plants, boy. What doctors in big cities don't mention much." She stopped, laughed to herself.

"There's folks with names who aim to start organizing and they wants all doctors to stop using what nature give us for help when the body goes bad. Fools is cutting off half our knowledge, supposed to be the mark of a civilization 'stead of us humans using what God gave us."

And there was Jacob, his arm fitted around the woman's shoulder, close to her face, and Mack saw the differences in their colors.

ABRUPT

Jacob had his own version; "It's called...she's a curandera. You got the weakness, she got a cure. Most times."

Husband and wife leaned on each other, the woman's hand rose to clasp the big paw belonging to Jacob. "Yes boy, this be why you sleep in the barn. No room in here for nothing but herbs."

Jacob led him to the barn. Deep in the back, under a crude set of stairs, there was a cot with blankets and even a sort of pillow. Jacob of course explained; "My wife, my Letty, she puts herbs in that pillow. Says anyone come by to sleep here, they be on the road and she wants to give them strength and fortitude. Nothin' special, she says, just herbs to help 'em along."

Then he smiled, and when Mack risked a look, the boy could see a difference in Jacob's manner.

"She's special, my Letty. She's part Indian and they teaches her about herbs. She listens and she knows." Then his face turned more familiar, not soft and sweet like when he talked of 'his Letty.' "Pump's to the barn back, you clean up and come for a meal. She knows you're a traveling man, you be always hungry. Come to the house, hear?"

Jacob and Letty left no room to argue.

LETTY'S COOKING WAS mostly unfamiliar names and green foods roasted in fat, meat that in Mack's mind was underdone even though it tasted good, so he grinned and ate what he could and said 'no thanks, ma'am' when more was offered.

Then, between the main meal and something sweet that posed as dessert, Letty excused herself, said she'd be right back and Jacob asked a few question about where Mack had come from, and why was he up here in the middle of nowhere. Mack in turn asked Jacob about that 1916 or thereabouts Chevy truck parked in the yard, muddied and loaded with shovels and a pick ax

Jacob called the truck a longtail, Mack countered with the color being faded green and how did Jacob come to own such a gift.

The Letty came back, wiping her hands, and there were fresh berries and warmed cream, a treat Mack did not expect.

LETTY SMILED AND said she'd refreshed the cot in the barn for him. No trouble, she said, it was a pleasure being able to treat him. As if she knew there was a flaw in Mack he could not hide.

Her gentle smile as Mack thanked her, for the meal and a cot in the bar, blinded him to whatever she might have done. He didn't care; he was tired.

THE NARROW COT was comfortable, he could shift and wiggle and the sweet smell from the frayed pillow let him sleep almost immediately.

He woke with his face pressed into the pillow; he was sobbing, unexpected and sad, emotions he tried to avoid. Feelings he had denied seemed to rise up inside him, a compound of terror at what awaited him, a death leaving life as too risky, too unknown. And deep inside he cried for his father, left behind, knowing that his only son had walked off in anger.

Mack did not understand why he cried; tears had not been his response before this terrible night. He rolled over, buried his face again in the sweet pillow and sobbed louder. Until he gulped, coughed, felt the staggered beat of his encased heart and wanted to scream. No! Not now.

Mack hiccupped, rolled his head on the pillow, sighed again, wiped his face and went back to sleep.

In the morning, as Mack shared coffee and eggs and fresh bread with the people, Letty smiled; "You had dreams last night. Them were good for you."

THEY FINISHED BREAKFAST in silence, then Mack went outside, not back to the barn but to stand and watch the sky and enjoy what was beautiful about taking in a deep breath of clear air.

Letty turned to her husband, hugging him from the back and resting her head on a shoulder. "I put fresh herbs in his pillow for last night. He's sad, Jacob, and there's more wrong. The herb...it helped the boy grieve. I would not want to have been inside the barn last night. I couldn't sleep...could hear him and the sound, it was...terrible."

Jacob turned and hugged his wife. "We need to get to work. The boy and me." They both smiled.

ABRUPT

fifteen

The truck was a 1915 Chevy longtail. Mack consoled himself 'cause he'd been off a year and Jacob laughed. The unexpected sound made Mack jump, then he too laughed.

"Where you'd get that ole truck?" Jacob wiped his face; "Gentleman was broke and I helped him take a burnt-out old shack to a dump. Paid me he did with this truck. "

MACK KNEW HE would do whatever Jacob told him. Riding in the odd vehicle was a rough treat; the longtail truck bed was filled with tools that rattled and banged as Jacob drove too fast and laughed each time the truck hit a bump.

Pick up downed tree limbs, cut and rake a lawn, help dispose of an old pet, get a bear cub down from a roof; no matter how small or dirty the chore was, Jacob went at his work with a cheerful manner.

Mack quickly learned to do what he was asked, don't argue with the clients. Jacob occasionally nodded to Mack as if in mild approval.

Come late afternoon, or the end of a particular chore, Jacob accepted whatever hard cash and a few live chickens, always a mess of apples, and thanked the giver.

Mack liked to study folks, do what he said he'd do, and there was a good meal, good company and a place for him to sleep at night.

Nothing stopped the questions forming in his mind; he'd thought that his terrible knowing, the illness that invaded his flesh and made the small incidences of life so important would be enough. Questions gave a ragged immortality denied him even as it shortened his life.

"Where were you born, Jacob?" A small and common question even as the facts were none of Mack's business. He already wanted the answer to another question; how did these two people meet. It was nobody's business and still Mack asked the question.

Jacob of course laughed; "That question you asked me, we first met. My family came to Nicodemus in Kansas and that is where I was born. I will not tell you how long ago." He laughed again, as if creating a place between sounds where he could speak a truth before beginning and ending to stop Mack's question.

The unspoken words were inevitable; "Mrs. Jacob, ah...Richardson, how did you meet her?" There was no laughter this time, no attempt to dissuade Mack. Jacob's face was stern, allowing no emotion, no satisfied curiosity.

"I tole you, boy. No more questions." Then Letty pushed herself past her husband, a move done kindly, while becoming a statement of her own; "I will answer, when you tell me, not Jacob, what is the hole you carry that so badly colors the life you lead."

This moment became a place Mack did not ever want to inhabit. He stepped back, felt his hands contract into fists. Then stopped, realized what he'd done by speaking out loud what had momentarily kept his attention.

"Ma'am, none of my business, either question." He sighed, searching for words as he tried to breathe but his chest was tight and he coughed, wanted to spit but there was no place nearby so he swallowed and the act hurt.

Letty Richardson stopped him, actually put a hand to his mouth. "There it is, your breathing. Tell me. Words out loud cannot hurt you. But what you do...it's wrong."

Mack looked to Jacob who shook his head; "Boy, there's no winning now."

SILENCE WHERE THE smallest sound of rapid breathing was the only movement; the harsh whisper through Mack's mouth was mimicked by both husband and wife. Mack's throat closed, he could not draw enough air to create an answer.

Letty touched his right hand, then stroked his chest, murmuring odd sounds as Mack struggled. He could make some sense of her words. "Easy...air...you're safe...I know."

Her hand came to rest on him and he could look down, see the roughened colors in her knuckles where they folded over his chest.

"Ma'am." He wanted to cry. "Ma'am, somethin' went wrong and two older brothers they each died afore a year old. I come along and showed those same signs killed the babies and my ma left. Ah hell."

That silence again, three of them quiet, no restless moves, no sighs or interrupting coughs. Then, from Mack, spoken in slow and indistinct words; "Was eighteen and went to join up on my own dime. Wasn't good enough, not even to die fighting. Their docs laughed and told me to go home and wait, it wouldn't be long." Silence again, as if the two watching him would make no noise to stop what he might say.

"Told me, my lungs and heart...not good." He watched her hand as it lightly rubbed where disaster waited. "My pa knew and never told me so I left. Been goin' some place or other since. Don't know, just sometimes I can't catch a breath."

That silence again, then the woman's sweet commanding voice. "There are herbs to help you, Mack. Please...."

BITTER, HARSH, A few with a delicate sweetness but always medicinal and Mack drank what he was given, rejoicing that something could be done.

He worked with Jacob, came home to find a brew waiting for him. Home became a new word, a place where he was greeted and tended to, even if he dared to say it, a place where he was loved.

Come November and Jacob talked endlessly 'bout what Letty would be cooking up for a meal, to celebrate what was given to each of them. A celebration from the Great

Emancipator, to any and all who would benefit from the abundance before them.

Driving to the small homestead where a good woman and a fine meal wait for these men gone out into the world to work and be rewarded had become a new satisfaction, enjoyed by Jacob Richardson and his helper, a shy, recovering child whose skin was white, who lived with a black man and a half-Osage woman with soft coffee skin; to the outside their life was peculiar. To each of them, life at that moment approached perfection.

And then, on a windy day, approaching an early dark, Jacob and Mack returned from hard and long work. Jacob sent Mack to feed the stalled animals in the barn, while he approached the house, where no cooking smells came from the dark kitchen.

No one greeted him at the door, no warm kiss and a giggle when he half-picked her up, no fresh bread cooling on the table. Nothing.

MACK FOUND HER lying near the colt's stall while the colt crowded in near the objecting mule. She was splayed out on the dusty floor, skirt to her hips, darkened exposed legs crossed, blood as a halo around her head eyes looking up, blinded by a deep gouge on her forehead.

Death gaped from her frozen mouth. Mack had not seen this death before; a loved one, a woman who cared. Then he heard Jacob's call, and moved to the corpse, where carefully, with eyes averted, Mack pulled the torn skirts down to cover the soft, bared ankles. One ankle had turned; its foot dangling from torn ligaments. The tenderness of her last moments was in front of him, a strong kick, an ankle turned under her, a terrible bleed-out and then death.

It could not be said who had done the killing; the mule who stolidly continued to eat dusty hay, or the restless dun colt.

Mack went back outside and caught Jacob as he started to pull at the barn door. "Don't, don't go in there." And once spoken out loud, the words could not be changed. "She's dead."

ABRUPT

sixteen

Jacob stood over his wife's body; no tears, no words at all. He did not look up at Mack, he did not glance at the mule and the suddenly-quiet dun colt. He waved at Mack as if the boy was a pesky fly. Mack went to the dark house, found a lantern near the door and lit its wick. Electricity had yet to come out onto the prairie and light up the outskirts of small towns.

His hands knew; reheat cold bacon, add spiced beans, fold a tortilla, a spoonful of green chile to the side. Looked all right, he decided, and carried the unsteady plate toward the barn.

Inside was what he expected; Jacob sat leaning on a post. His wife, his dead wife, had been pulled to rest in Jacob's lap. Smeared blood darkened the stable boards, the two animals chewed their evening hay. Flies buzzed at Letty's head, walked along the drying stream of her blood and Jacob did not care.

Mack knelt down carefully, positioned the plate of food near Jacob's hand, and gently took the woman's stiffened body in both hands, pulling her corpse free of Jacob's embrace. He allowed her body to lie quietly in an unused stall, covered with a loudly-striped saddle blanket.

In the barn's shadows, Mack stepped into the underneath of the loft stairs and sat on the cot. Only then did he cry. Not loud sobs that would interrupt Jacob's mourning, but his own quiet tribute to a woman gracious enough to accept his failings.

MACK DIDN'T KNOW when Jacob took the new corpse out behind the barn to dispose of what was now only degrading flesh. Sleep was the only place where Mack was freed from the specter of Letty Richardson.

At daylight, Mack fed the dun, went back and fed the mule, packed what little gear belonged to him, and left the barn and the sadness that haunted him. He could not imagine how Jacob would manage without his wife, so he ran. Pointed the dun colt north and rode out at dawn, refusing to consider what he left behind.

JACOB RICHARDSON HAD buried his wife; now he needed to cook his own meals, work where he was needed, thank people who'd come looking for Letty's help and learned of her death.

He needed to do these things, to make himself go on. Instead he sat, hungry for her, uninterested in food. Drinking short sips of water, letting the herbs in that terrible room wilt and die.

After several folks came by, wanting one thing or another and were sent away by an angry Jacob, the lost and lonely man turned the mule loose, left keys in the 1915 Chevy faded green, longtail truck, and walked out onto the prairie beyond the small town where for seven good years he and his woman made their life.

ABRUPT

Mack never looked back. Only a few days into his escape, he found it hard to breathe, and his heart could quit its rhythm on a whim, long enough to frighten him.

seventeen

A snowflake hit his nose, melting immediately before more snowflakes covered his face, hat, the show of long curls around his neck. Snow. He pulled up the dun and let more snow pour over them. In the distance he could follow the snow-filled dirt track of two cars heading north, a brand new truck coming south, headed toward the small town Mack had just left.

Oh yes, snow, meant it was coming to Christmas and a long winter, always cold and yet Mack was headed north. Stupid.

Then he remembered; the dead woman, Jacob's sorrow. Blood still a shadow on Mack's hands. He guided the dun colt into a walk, then a slow jog, and saw that another truck was riding the crest of the road going north, reminding Mack he was in the wrong century, clothed in old clothes and riding a damn horse into the snow.

With nothing left, no place specific to go, Mack pointed the colt to an island of trees where they could wait out the storm. It wasn't much, a few gathering of lean leafless aspens, an old dried-out juniper skeleton and enough twisted branches that the colt and Mack covered themselves, shivered, and waited for daylight.

MACK WOKE WHEN the colt whinnied. Confused, cold, worried about the dun colt, Mack sat up quickly, aware he was hungry. Aware too that the colt had been busy stripping leaves and even bark from their night's poor accommodations, Mack coughed as cold air directly reached his lungs. He tried to stand but coughing doubled him over. On his knees, mucus and phlegm dripping from his mouth, he saw strips of red in the expelled and thickened liquid.

Blood. Mack bit his lip to stop that liquid, to hide from a too recent memory of a woman's bloodied face. He shut his eyes, absolutely refused to cough. Then a sense of movement opened his eyes and he could see two black hooves much too close to his nose. Damn, he thought. The foolish dun colt.

A bout of coughing was the answer. The colt stepped back, nervous, blowing through distended nostrils. "S'all right, kid." Mack tried soothing the horse who would have none of it. More steps backward until the colt was caught up by a tied rein so the colt swung sideways, exposing Mack to the restless hind legs.

Ugly instinct grabbed at Mack; on hands and knees he scurried through the snow-covered brush, far away from those threatening hind legs. Then he stopped and laughed, coughed some and laughed even more.

IT HAD STOPPED snowing, that much was clear. Blowing clouds cleared the sky and reminded Mack he couldn't make a meal off the aspen bark like the dun colt. Damn but he was hungry; he sat back and lifted his head and from the new viewpoint there was nothing to offer a man any type of sustenance. He laughed again, a dry humorless sound. Hell, he thought, dying before my time ain't what I expected.

And there was no one to hear his thoughts.

Behind him the colt kicked out, then called, and called again when nothing answered. On the third call, a distant horse answered and Mack froze, listened, and the unseen horse called again. Mack smiled.

A SPECK IN the distance moved quickly, growing larger even as Mack stood up, went back for the colt tangled in its own reins, cactus caught in its tail.

He was ready to climb onto the colt when the horse and rider came into the small stand of trees. "Well, boy, good mornin' to you." Mack steadied the dun, turned to the greeting; "Mornin'."

An old man, hunched over the horn of an old-style, hard-used saddle. "Been tryin to figure what hid in this here copse of trees. Heard a horse call, feared I might be missin' a bronc or two."

Silence, as Mack sorted through what the old man could mean. Then he grinned; "One good thing 'bout this colt, his color ain't that common. You know by now that the colt's not one of yours."

The returned grin from the old man was truly a miracle; a mass of wrinkles and tired muscles moved the gray-whiskered face into a gargoyle's leer meant to be comic.

Mack could only shake his head. "Yes sir. The colt's mine."

"Good. Now looks to me you could use some grub. Come on, tighten up that colt's cinch and follow 'long." The invitation to a meal was enough, still Mack wondered; he wasn't much more than a half-baked kid, almost illiterate, few skills, lousy health and sure 'nuff not much to look at. Still the old man aimed at a distant point only he could see, and for the lack of any other direction, Mack followed. He kept the colt to a good distance behind the old man's horse, which had seemed too willing to kick out in the beginning.

The old man pulled up his sorrel and waited; "Sonny what you doin' out here when it's damn cold 'nuff you could freeze, you and that ornery colt."

Any answer exposed Mack's stupidity so he sighed and told a miserable truth, shaking his head with each word; "Was death, old man. Two times and nothin' I did or could do. An absentee owner, then a man's wife. Couldn't do nothin' but leave, both times."

Almost a lie, he thought, but too complicated to explain, so Mack let his head drop, his gaze counted a few blades of dried grass showing through trampled snow, and he waited.

"Okay, you come work or me. Do what I tells you and we'll last out the winter." That was all the old man had to say.

MACK LEARNED QUICKLY to accept the silence, live within the boundaries and get on with the chores. The shack was warm, a well outside gave up clear water, and the things needed doing for the livestock were routine, chores Mack could do without thinking.

The work never pushed Mack beyond his limit. The old man's expectations were lowered by his age. For Mack it was a blessing, he could finish a day's chores without exhaustion or an empty sense of his own being. Carl Carhart, that was the old man's name, was accepting of what Mack could do, making the uneven partnership into a comfortable daily routine.

One morning, looking out to melting snow and a bright sun overhead, the old man shook his head. "Gonna be them babies comin' soon. Got our work cut out." Somewhere, Mack figure, some time, Christmas had skipped out of his world. No loss since he wasn't much for celebrating.

OLD MAN CARHART was strong on work and uninterested in talk. Mack was given a stout bay mare and they went out to circle the herd, check on cows getting' ready to birth.

Mack rode behind the cowman and marveled at the numbers the two men found, hidden in arroyos or lying down in the new grass. Multiples of cows, most bagged up and ready to calve.

"Mr. Carhart you got a lot of ladies here." He didn't know how to explain. "Yep, boy, got me a life's work here."

That answer wasn't enough for Mack. He opened his mouth and Carhart pulled up his sorrel gelding, spun the horse around. "Boy, them's my ladies. You do what I say, you can stay."

By June all the female cattle were joined by small replicas of themselves and Mack's 23rd birthday had come and gone without notice. Mack wasn't much taken with the beeves. They might be money on the hoof to the old man but for Mack they represented the wide world that meant little balanced against the sentence directing Mack's life.

After a last inspection of the ever-growing useless herd, Carhart rode to the meager ranch, turned the sorrel out and gestured to Mack to do the same. Then the old man stamped into the shack and when Mack followed, the old man was pulling hard on an unmarked liquor bottle, a quarter gone and the old man showed no sign of quitting.

Mack went to what passed for his room; what had once been a closet where bridles, broken reins, torn stirrup fenders and whatever might sometime need repair, were stored until the old man found the time.

He sat on the rough-covered mattress, and considered what might happen next. Never had seen the old man drink and Mack didn't like it. Nothing he could do, even as the drinking was a bad sign.

THEN MR. CARHART filled the doorway and Mack stood up. "Yeah?" The old man grinned, showing three teeth missing on the upper left, and one front tooth without its mate.

"You got youself a sweet way, kid. And I got a need. All that feed and sleep for the winter, I want my payback now." Mack felt a shiver go up his back to his neck. Then Carhart lost his advantage by stepping back.

"Old man, I ain't giving you nothing. Get out, now." Mack didn't know where the strength of anger came from but he would not give up himself. He raised both fists, clenched in fury, and the old man tried again, coming in close to Mack until the two men could stare at each other, until Mack held firm and shook his head. Carhart sighed and left.

Mack disappeared that night, clothes and utensils rolled up in his blanket. The old man sat in front of the cold wood stove and said nothing.

Mack dozed in the saddle while the dun again traveled north. Seemed like all he could do was run.

ABRUPT

eighteen

He woke to a pounding heart and lungs gasping for rain-filled air. Mack was drenched, water running down his back, bare hands cold and stiff around saddle swell. When it was time, when the sun thinned and dried the heavy air, at first peeking through gray clouds, slowly moving thickened air until the sun had a full blue sky to lighten. Only then did Mack have a renewed energy that allowed him to dismount from the dun and stand on his own two legs.

Now he could see the horse, exposed ribs, hair loose in patches; a cruelty Mack would never expect from himself. The dun had been part of Mack's escape, and the horse showed its poor existence.

No room for logic or good sense; Mack was careful of the dun as he pulled the saddle loose from the ridged back, dropped it onto the ground. No care, no bother, let the saddle land on cactus, burrs that immediately hung on the saddle blanket. Mack couldn't care, he intended to discard everything connected with the old-fashioned rig.

When he very carefully pulled the headstall off the dun and the horse stood, isolated, naked, half-starved. Mack waved a hand and the dun turned away, realized a new freedom and trotted toward a distance Mack couldn't see. Suddenly, tail high, head raised, the dun leaped into an awkward gallop, and in that simple, quick moment,

Mack indeed left a life behind and stepped into a new century.

THE HORSE WAS long out of sight. A double set of tires across hard snow was the only man-made structure Mack could see. To his right there was a high, hollow rise; to the left, far away, there were mountain peaks covered with more snow. Interwoven and stark, the mountain presented a barrier Mack did not want to approach.

On foot, tired, and always hungry, Mack freed his bed roll from the useless saddle and headed east, following a dirt track around the core of a singular mountain

To his surprise, Mack found he was grinning and he stopped, looked back to see the hollowed mountain, rising as if it was the symbol of his past. Still grinning, he looked toward the east, to where he though Kansas lurked, flat and blowing, as enough people had told him. Out there was the small town he didn't want to see. Nicodemus, the birth place for Jacob, and Letty. As he carried their memory, he saw them alive. Not dead, never dead if he kept that moment closed.

He didn't want to know their beginning. Mack shook, turned more north and angled himself toward trees and the promise of higher ground, hidden lands holding no memories that could hurt.

He followed a road, stumbled across frozen ruts, caught one boot heel in a hoof print before stepping high over a thin tire print. The road held remnants of travel so the choice to follow the track took on an unexpected importance. His breathing was shallow, he could feel skin heat from a rising fever and by God he was hungry past all good sense. The road, showing hard travel, would lead him to food. He had no other hope.

DESPITE TIME SPENT on the road, his surroundings never changed. Rocky ground, thin green plants filled with thorns, blue sky with few clouds. Hot despite a gusty wind, with no place to hide under a cool tree.

A faint noise, far behind him, drew Mack's attention. The noise grew louder; he turned, curious about the growing racket and it was an automobile, enveloped in a dry cloud of raised dust.

This was new to Mack's experience; he was startled by the approaching vehicle's speed and the weight of dust it kicked up. When the automobile was almost next to him, still going too fast, he had to jump back, tripped over a dried-out track and ended up on his back, quickly covered with more dust.

He sat up in time to watch the vehicle pull away from him. An arm was stuck in the air, the hand waved back at him, then once more held on to the wheel and the vehicle seemed to pick up speed.

Walking in the middle of the road, once again alone, Mack coughed lightly from the raised dust, then quickly sank to his knees, coughing harder, struggling for breath.

Five minutes, more coughing, a few minutes of rest and Mack could stand.

Eventually he walked on, slowly, cautious not to push even as he was more determined to reach a destination. As the dust settled, the air cleared and Mack could trace the vehicle's path far into the distance.

Then the dust stopped, at what seemed to be the end of a curve. Mack kept walking, mildly curious. There was no evidence of a ranch in the long valley ahead of him, but an entrance to a house or barn could be out there and difficult to see until he was almost on top of the shallow turn.

HE STOPPED FOR a rest twice before the land dipped into a long valley. No sign of dust led him; he walked out of stubbornness, on rare occasions he stopped and coughed, then continued walking.

Yes. There was a barely used track meeting with the main road. And even from this distance, Mack saw the rear end of a vehicle hanging off a steep corner. He tried to hurry. At each step, cries came from the hanging vehicle.

Breathing hard, stopping to let his breathing settle, a shrill cry startled Mack into moving. Forward and fast; he collided with the vehicle's upended rear, one tire spinning in empty space, the other jammed to the rim in arroyo dirt.

Mack skidded down the car's right side to the passenger door. Grabbing hold of the vehicle's doors, he spun on one foot while trying to grab anything to hold him. Dust rose quickly, he coughed and his chest hurt.

Leaning into the body of the car, he touched flesh and something screamed.

He jerked away, looked at his hand and the fingers were blood-covered. A low moan came from the front seat, then a wet cough spraying the driver and Mack.

Only then did Mack realize the hanging car had moved sideways, threatening to dislodge itself from the edge and fall. Bottom of the arroyo looked to be too far and Mack didn't like what had to happen next.

A shoulder and a bloody arm hit out at Mack, smearing liquid on his face as he grabbed for any part of the inhabitant. He was slapped, then a leg still wearing heels kicked at Mack, dislodging his grip on the woman's ribs.

Fighting each other, Mack pulling hard, the injured woman resisted, digging cruelly at Mack's side. Two intertwined figures slid from the car as its bulk twisted and with little warning dropped off the edge.

There was a moment when Mack felt the woman slide free of him and he dug deep into what was left, yanked her back onto him as he fell into weeds and the deep gouges of car tracks.

The outside world was too quiet; the woman lay diagonally across Mack, her breathing shallow, her eyes tightly closed. Under her, Mack sprawled out, pushed into loosened sand and unable to get the woman off him.

Mack heard nothing but heavy breathing, until a face leered at him, a hand reached down, two more hands lifted the girl from him and he was meant to grip the offered hand and pull himself free. Mack smiled politely; "Let me...." Later he remembered rolling part way over, starting to rise and then...nothing.

nineteen

"Why did you rescue her?" The question needed some time to consider. Mack had to open his eyes and see who was asking with such hidden cruelty. The answer was quite simple; as if Mack could see what was before him and do nothing.

"Why?" Insistent son, Mack thought. He drew in air, ready to answer, and only a cough came out, barking and painful and he couldn't stop until the unseen speaker rolled Mack on his side and waited.

It seemed that even coming to an injured person's aid did not excuse him from the forces directing Mack's life. He coughed again. Two hands pulled him up to sitting against a pillow and only then could Mack spit out phlegm as another hand wiped his mouth.

With all the fuss going on, Mack composed his answer as he was turned and manipulated and moved into a more convenient place. The room itself was small, dark, furnished with a single bed, a slat-back chair, no rugs or curtain. Hired hand, most likely Mack thought. Back of the house. Where he belonged.

"Couldn't leave her...." Here he stopped, felt a sudden internal pounding and the words were gone, but only for a moment. "Blood, never good. And the automobile...it fell."

Mack crumpled down against the pillow and closed his eyes.

HER FATHER STEPPED back to stand beside his daughter. She sat in a new wooden chair on wheels, and wore bandages on her extended leg and one hand. A sticking plaster covered her left eye and ear.

"He gave us little information to help understand his motives. It seems his actions went against whatever torments him so. I know, Dr. Montgomery told me he really did not expect the boy to survive." The tall man, dressed properly in twill pants and an ironed white shirt, was careful not to look at his daughter as he told her what the doctor had said. And each time he spoke about the young man, never using his name, the emphasis on 'his' or 'the boy' carried a most unpleasant quality.

"Papa, why does it matter what his motives were? Despite all expectations, I am alive and it seems that my savior will live. We deserve a celebration, not condemnation."

AS IF HE wasn't there, his life had no meaning. He kept his eyes closed even as his mind raced, bouncing from their reality to what he already knew. Mack had learned that what he was gave him no exception from emotion.

The words spoken over and around Mack, carrying little sympathy to remind him of his place, served as a goad to defend himself. His voice was roughened, harsh; "Your daughter...child. She was hurt. That's all, hurt." His voice quit, he panted for air.

What came next from Mack was ugly; "Listen to her, you're her father. She's alive. Who the hell cares who I am or...what's my reason." Right here he had to stop, even knowing that the rest needed to be said. Words, even the sound needed to speak them, were tearing into him. "She has life again. Treasure her." That was enough, all that was possible. This time Mack truly slept, exhausted by each syllable.

The next time Mack was completely awake, a doctor stood at the foot of his bed and the angry father was half-way out the door.

"Good, you're awake and seem to be doing quite well. Sleeping for this long has been good for you." Then there was a break in the doctor's bright patter. The man almost gone from Mack's room stopped and turned, his voice angry; "Why'd you...?"

Mack smiled and it didn't hurt, he didn't want to cough or even close his eyes. "Told you once. Your girl...too much blood." He discovered that even now there was an internal pain attached to his words. "Anyone finding her...would do the same."

The girl's father left, shaking his head. The doctor hesitated; "Mister...ah, Mack. From my tests and observation, you have several handicaps so why did you go to Elizabeth's rescue?"

No one could hear the simple words of Mack's explanation. "Because she was in trouble." The doctor seemed to be smiling. "Young man, given your limitations, which you obviously understand, what you have done is truly remarkable. And I don't think Mr. McAlester or his daughter for that matter, I don't believe they can comprehend the value of what you've done. As for me, I realize the entire situation is impossible to understand, yet it's what you did and I admire your courage under the circumstances. That's all."

An odd compliment, Mack thought. But well meant. And then he was back asleep.

WHEN MACK PUT both feet on the floor, took a deep breath and stood, he immediately fell on his face. No time to even get his hands out to soften the fall.

Close up, the planed wood floor was an intersection of growth lines and saw cuts. Scuffed in places, indents of foot traffic headed toward the door. Side of the bed the color had been worn away, from sitting up with feet wide apart on the floor. What Mack had attempted before he stood up. Too damn soon.

Then wheels came close to his head and he objected out loud. A young woman's voice had an answer; "Well what else can I do? My father is out, then again he'd be no help in this situation, now would he."

Mack grunted; he studied the wheelchair, the heavy wheels, the fact that her leg was no longer in a cast but sat on a foot rest, as did the uninjured leg.

"Ma'am." He heard her intake of breath. "Miss, if I can grab the armrests, I could pull myself up to standing. Wouldn't be polite, miss, but it could be done."

She gave her consent, then told him; "Sir, when you rescued me, neither of us stood on ceremony. Grab where you must and believe me I will smile and be glad to help."

Reaching in between her legs, then grabbing for each armrest, Mack found himself closer than comfortable with another human being. He would have been this close with his mother, and she was long gone. And he'd always been too young to remember.

The girls behind him were a long line of missed or refused chances. He couldn't give in to any attraction. Consequently he had no skills to count on. Usually he just kept going. Better than having to explain.

Not this time. He needed her wheelchair, with her weight in it to help keep a stability while Mack climbed to his feet.

She was a good sort. Elizabeth McAlester, that was her name, and Mack wasn't uncomfortable around her. They'd been here before.

Not being able to see beneath his chest, Mack felt the softness of her skin as he grabbed for the armrests. Only a moment, for both of them, there was a gentle, tactile sensation until she pulled her arms free from his unintended caress. Elizabeth smiled and Mack was close enough he could feel the movement around her mouth.

"Yes, miss." Then an expulsion of his breath. "Sorry." She countered with; "We agreed, no apologies or explanations." Mack had to grin and the girl smiled again. "It's different. Mack." He wanted to agree.

In order to stand up, Mack had to draw his torso higher, to be on the level with his hands. Which ended with Mack leaning his weight on her chest, with his upper thighs coming down into her lap. Despite the awkward contact, and the warnings Mack knew too well, his body reacted as organically intended.

"Miss, I didn't..." "Mack, did you know you're quite beautiful, especially this close." Again he could feel movement in her face and looked away, feeling heat rise from his own body. "Mack, despite what my father thinks, I'm not inexperienced. Whatever it is you want...oh." As if she remembered.

"I want...well thank you. I can't..." She kissed his cheek, then his mouth. Very gently as if bestowing a gift.

Now he knew and what was offered became a torment. As if she herself knew, she had to know, Elizabeth pulled herself back into the wheelchair, closed her mouth, and removed herself from their contact.

Mack's visceral response shocked him even as the intensity of immediate pleasure made him want more. Wanting what other men accepted as their right.

With a harsh discipline honed over years of deprivation, Mack refused his body's signals and found himself breathing hard, heart thumping loud enough the young woman touched his chest and she was crying.

"So unfair." Her soft voice and its tremor, the hint of tears on her face, almost brought Mack to climax. His frame shook; his hands gripped the arm rest, he reared back, lost his balance and threw himself onto the bed. Flat on his back, too aware of his slowly-diminishing erection, Mack was exposed and vulnerable.

Elizabeth cautioned him; "My father is coming down the back hall. Quick, sit up. Nothing's happened, nothing will happen."

WHEN MR. MCALESTER stood at the doorway and grunted, his daughter nodded and smiled, and Mack stood, unbalanced but upright. "Afternoon, your daughter arrived to make me go for a walk with her."

McAlester shook his head, turned and disappeared. Wordless and humiliated, Mack stepped behind Elizabeth's wheelchair and moved her as she directed.

There was a door at the end of the hall. In the other direction was the kitchen; in there Mack had on occasion enjoyed the cooking smells. Either way was a freedom Mack had missed.

HE WOKE FROM a dream early the next morning. A woman had come to him, soft and glowing, reaching for him, and only now did he feel her flesh, know what she wanted. He woke before the inevitable conclusion but this time he knew what he'd lost.

twenty

He now occupied a world previously unknown to him. The home was his first three-story house, even thought he slept in a down-stairs back room intended for a servant girl.

Outside there were gardeners in charge of the great lawn and a spread of flowers to please the owners. That Mr. John McAlester could possibly enjoy both the scent and colors of these plantings was enough to further confuse Mack.

There were an overabundance of house servants, upstairs maids and a cook, a man to shovel coal and maintain the radically new furnace which warmed the house in winter and sometime produced hot water on demand.

All these people were employed to keep one man, a widower, and his daughter not quite twenty years old, to keep these people marginally comfortable in a fancy house outside the New Mexico-Colorado border, when the nearest big settlement was Trinidad to the west in Colorado, and Folsum, New Mexico closer and to the east.

Inserted into the mix simply because he had saved the daughter further pain and suffering, Mack, just Mack, no last name ever offered, had a place; a room, a job when he chose it, a reason for his existence.

The change was for an odd reason; unpredictably, Mack became the companion to Miss Elizabeth. She enjoyed his company and no longer had time to fight with her father or try to run away when going to a school for ladies, to learn deportment and good manners, was her certain future.

"MACK, I WISH to spend time in the south garden. Would you push me, and ask the cook to prepare a picnic lunch?" An order spoken politely, as if the request would naturally include Mack in the celebration.

An underlying indifference was part of the treatment by numerous servants, whose initial reaction had been crude and unpleasant. Mack would give no last name; therefore Mack was running from the law, or a wife, or something so ugly that he would never discuss his past.

Putting Mack in conflict with the cook left a smile on Elizabeth's face. She loved confrontation especially if it included anyone but her.

To Elizabeth, Mack's unmentioned handicaps added a certain sinister dimension that bothered her father and consequently pleased his daughter.

MACK LEARNED NOT to expect much from the McAlesters, father and daughter. He slept well, was fed three meals a day, and had access to whatever was shoved into the fridge.

He also knew there was nothing keeping Elizabeth in the wheelchair. She could walk, often did inside the garden when her father was away and the staff used the time to act as they chose, without supervision.

He said nothing, not to Elizabeth even as she stood over him, and he never betrayed her to her father, for that would be giving the old man ammunition forcing her to become herself and not an invalid daughter.

This time, the cook's lunch was fresh bread and hand-churned butter, a jar of pickles, thinly-sliced ham, mild mustard, a bottle of iced tea, silverware and crystal glasses. A small feast, ending with warm gingerbread smothered with a soft creamed icing.

Perfection; except for the lies, the anger between father and daughter, and the pain of living that lie.

WELL-RESTED, REVIVED by time, Mack felt as if the past had dissolved in sleep. If this was how a normal male felt, he could understand what he'd missed, and planned on how he could refashion what had passed by him.

First on his list was the continuation of the stunning moment when he was supported by Elizabeth's body and how he felt. He could link that pleasure to all the females he'd walked away from, fearful that remaining with them would quite literally dissolve and destroy him.

He didn't feel that way now; his lungs worked, his heart beat a constant, comforting rhythm leaving Mack with little to fear.

Freedom must taste this way; freedom to do what he chose.

Right now, he would have a woman, to find out the limit to what he'd been missing.

SHE MUST HAVE sensed a difference in him. Now her hand lingered on him wherever she could reach. Long fingers, curled slightly, stroking the back of a hand, head rested against his upper thigh, a faint sigh. Signals that would have sent him running now were his to act on if he chose. She was no innocent, not like her father assumed her to be. He would wonder even as he didn't care. She was telling him, and Mack had tasted just enough to anticipate what waited.

It was a matter of her father away on an undefined business, the staff otherwise occupied, and Elizabeth being willing to join him in hired servant's bed.

Then one morning, all his hopes were blown apart, by the sound of his lungs, the incredible pain in his chest, that drove all thoughts from him except to breathe in shallow gasps, and half-sit up to remove pressure from his heart.

He had been dreaming of Elizabeth and now his clothing stuck to his thighs, his groin ached pleasantly and he was ashamed even before he realized what had happened.

Pleasure given and then taken away before Mack could explore what he barely understood.

Now the sense between them became unforgiving. Elizabeth was filled with orders;

she would go here, or for a drive, to the garden for a solitary cup of tea. Soft hands no longer teased him, his dreams were a torment. Returned to his weakness, Mack had to make himself get up and work. Do as he was told, become a servant to Elizabeth's whim.

MACK WARNED HER first, that he would no longer join in the lie. Elizabeth half-rose from the chair and Mack thanked her for the recovery time, leaving Elizabeth stranded at the foot of stairs to the second floor. He went back to the hired hand's room, packed, and left the house to travel across a grazed pasture which joined the main road closer to the nearest town. He'd had enough.

Toward the day's end, Mack found out how easy life had been at the McAlester house. Now, tired, short of breath, he sat and waited.

He'd had a taste, a brief and unfinished break in his life, where what was seen as normal presented Mack with an ultimate truth.

If he was to go forward, there was a choice needing to be made. A choice Mack shied away from; ugly, harsh, necessary. He could walk himself into nothing, or he could live by confining rules and find out how far a man with two strikes against him could get. It was always Mack's dilemma, belonging to no one else.

He stood, awkward, sore now, that damnable short breath limiting energy and determination. To walk was next. He stood, swaying, panting. Then he was tired of the whole damned incident; thinking, planning, making peace with limits. He wanted to hit someone or something, glad now that he'd left the McAlester family behind or there would have been a fight.

Instead of going into the small town and finding some shack or local barn, Mack curled up against the base of a still-warm arroyo and slept without dreams.

twenty-one

He woke up hungry. The small warmth of the circled trees had given in to a dark night and now an early chill shivered through Mack's flesh and brittle bones. Waking hungry was accompanied by immediate despair.

By concentration and determination, Mack could stand, holding on to a smaller tree. "Hello." Mack flinched, could turn slowly and eventually he saw a small child, who looked up at him. "Hello." Her voice was soft, under-developed and shrill.

The adversary was a small child, wearing one shoe, a dress too small to button all the way up the front. The child smiled; the face wore dirt and smudges, the child's hands were skinned on the knuckles, fingernails too long, a dripping snub nose. She was a lost child out of place. Not a house in sight; Mack had no idea how the child got to his spot.

"Hello." As if this one word was her limit. Mack gripped one of the trees and knelt down, to look closely at the child. She smiled and reached out a grubby hand to touch Mack's cheek.

She was all the children, all the family and friends he could never have. He sighed and it turned into a coughing spell and her small hands came out to pat his face. Behind the cough, and the pain, Mack wanted to smile simply because a child tried to please him.

In exchange for her generous compassion, Mack could take her home. He stood and she looked up as if he was an exaggerated god and again he wanted to smile.

"Do you know where you've come from right now?" Mack hid behind another cough; how did those words jump out of his mouth? She was just a child. Still she pointed to a distant ridge, where the top of a bent chimney puffed out tired smoke in short gasps.

"There." Her face screwed up. "I think." It wasn't much to go on but he was surprised she knew a direction. Mack first checked her feet and she was missing one shoe but had both socks, dirty, falling at her ankles At least the tracks of one shoe, one sock could be easy to follow.

Then it came to Mack, that life at least for him was the simple things, such as this, a lost child with one shoe. There could not be much more, so the only solution was to treasure what he did have.

When they started in the direction of the smoldering chimney across an arroyo, the child took Mack's hand. The sticky touch of small fingers reminded Mack of how much he had missed. When he looked down, he was struck by the top of the child's head; hair pulled free of crude braiding, bright and thick light brown hair.

A tug on his hand and Mack stopped. Kneeling to be level with the child, she smiled at him and pointed in a vague direction.

Mack looked, towards an arroyo filled with a thin stream of dirty water.

The child's uneven tracks led toward a fenced house, a huge cottonwood tree, a loose-board barn and a small vegetable plot. Mack stood up, moving slowly as tired muscles tried to respond. "Child, you wait here. I need to pile up what little I've got, then we'll take you home."

As Mack turned, the child started to cry, as if he meant something to her. One more step away from her and the child cried louder. Mack went back, stood a moment, not knowing what to do.

Common sense and the foolishness of the situation brought him to kneel in front of the crying child. She smiled, Mack put his hands out and she moved into their safety, finally putting her head under his chin and they held the embrace.

Common sense had him lead the child back to his poor camp where he gathered his few belongings and they started again in the direction the child seemed to know.

TEN MINUTES LATER Mack stood at the door to a small adobe hut, bent down and knocked. He didn't know what else to do. The girl stood way back, holding to a broken juniper and watching.

A bent old man opened the door. "What you want? We got nothing to give you." He half-closed the door, then stopped. "What'd you do to her? Damn you."

An equally bent woman pushed the old man aside and walked hurriedly, with a distinct limp, toward the child. Mack stepped away, curious in a mildly detached way. Too much had happened; he was already tired.

The girl ran toward the old woman, her face wide in that fetching grin. "Mamam. Yes." The child's voice was enough to bring a smile to Mack's face.

He turned in time to see what the old man intended. A raised club hung loosely in the gnarled hands, the wood shiny where the old man held it. Then the club came down, aimed perfectly to connect with Mack.

Lacking any curiosity, Mack reached out and grabbed the club, twisted the smooth wood and took the weapon from the old man. Too easy, Mack thought, he was not that strong.

Then the old woman hit his shoulders, he ducked his head and shielded himself with two hands. The old woman kept hitting, the child cried, screaming at the old man and the woman, who kept pounding on Mack.

He straightened out and mindlessly yelled; the child grabbed one hand and yelled with Mack. The old woman stopped, the old man bowed his head. They were quiet, until a cur dog and two pups surrounded the three adults and the child, howling while their tails wagged.

Chaos, with no clear excuse.

The old man glared at Mack; the woman said; "How can you treat my child so? She is not right, you cannot play with her."

That was it, what Mack had understood in the child, a look that didn't see.

"Mamam, he brought me home. He's my friend. Papi, don't hurt him."

MACK LEFT TWO days later, well fed, wearing clean clothes that almost fit. Little had been said; the old couple fed Mack, the child smiled at him, half-hidden behind her grandmother's long shirt. Words were a premium in the family, rarely used except out of necessity..

No one tried to explain what had happened. Silence was the only answer, and Mack never tried to understand. He walked away, having no idea where he would end up.

.

ABRUPT

twenty-two

I've lost count; too many years filled with nothing but the same day, life consisting of feeding hunger, finding a safe place to sleep. Sometimes working for a year or two, or an afternoon, a week; most of the time getting caught in other folks' dreams and disasters; that I could leave was my salvation.

I did wander, satisfying curiosity as well as following where food and a job, a vague security, would take me. New Mexico was mostly ranch jobs, sometimes for a few days, a week; once or twice for a few years. I even drifted into Colorado, sticking mostly to the southeast corner of the state. A barren dusty place, with little call for the few talents I'd developed. Shoveling, nailing, picking crops, hauling dead tree limbs.

So I drifted again, time that was never wasted; time that had no meaning since I was never on track to a career, a common life others considered righteous and normal.

The following became my perfected skills. Two simple, unproductive learned behaviors: leaving, and reading. Over the few years, often burdened with empty time, I learned imperfectly to read. It became a way of life; finding an unknown word, saving it to ask a more knowledgeable person the meaning of this perplexing combination of letters. By doing this over and over, holding, questioning, finding someone to ask, I managed to amass a wildly-varied vocabulary despite my limited education and half-promised life span.

As for work, I was marginally capable of herding cattle, driving half-wrecked old cars, nailing up a few boards, building gates, digging ditches. All those chores no one else chose to do, so I got hired, or fed, given some kind of cheap reward for doing what no one else wanted. Cleaned out a pig sty several times, even dug a new pit and moved a privy, when rich city folks had indoor plumbing and country folk relied on a newly dug privy pit.

Sure I got tired, seemed like the time between sheer exhaustion and the bare ability to work was more and more exhaustion and less and less energy.

All this meant my chance for wealth or even a bowl of soup became less and less certain. A downward spiral; the weaker I became, it was less and less possible to earn anything, but mostly it meant less food, leaky accommodations, poor sleep. The downward spiral meant an ultimate end and I wasn't ready yet to give in, to fulfill the inevitable first pronouncement about my abbreviated future.

To hell with what had been said. I'm still alive and while my life has not followed the path of predictability, it's my life and it don't belong to anyone but me.

JUST BECAUSE HE could, Mack went east, over the New Mexico line into the Oklahoma panhandle; barren, few roads mostly dirt, wrecked cars to the road side or left to rust in weed-filled pastures.

He walked, no more horses for him. A big sign to any possible job or work, that he was still in the past, knew only cow work, nothing recent or modern. Rides were easy, a turned face, and thumb out as a signal and often a pick-up truck would stop, an older man would spit out the rolled-down window, then ask the obvious; 'you want a ride? Hop in." Sometimes it was the comfort of the cab, more often it was the open bed, with Mack braced up against the outside of the cab, wind-blown, but at least he didn't have to walk.

There could be a job, a meal, occasionally a place to sleep but these lasted a few days, no longer. Mack wasn't a kid anymore; age showed in his face, lines, wind-burn, matted gray curls plastered to his skull.

By his poor memory and record-keeping, Mack figured he would be twenty-seven next Tuesday. His late present this time was going through unknown country. New Mexico and Colorado had given up all they could, sheltering and hiding him for years.

The road across the panhandle went from dirt to a hard tarred surface. It let cars go faster but the shoulders raised hell on a man intending to walk. Dust, holes, pebbles in his shoes.

Then he laughed; stopped walking, dropped his bedroll and threw back his head.

Howled at the blue sky, laughter that went into coughing but he was still laughing. Complaining about dirt and rocks all the time he breathed mostly clean air and enjoyed a bright blue sky. His choice, and then he wanted to bitch and complain.

Quite a picture, Mack thought. A lone man, belongings at his feet, head raised to the sky. Two cars went past, seeming to move faster as they drove by a crazy man yelling at the universe.

He kept walking then, barely lifting the bedroll, not caring when the battered coffee pot banged on his leg at every stride..

A truck pulled to the side in front of him. A man's head stuck out of the rolled window; "Hey mister, you want a ride? Sure could use a good laugh."

It was a newer truck, pretty fancy according to Mack's estimation. The driver was pretty fancy too; a pressed white shirt, clean pants, boots free of mud and manure. And nestled up against the man was a young girl, the driver's daughter in Mack's private estimation.

"Well boy, you're out here in nowhere just laughing it up, walking wherever you want, no cares. None at all." The words came easy to the man, and behind them was a bitterness Mack didn't like. He could feel the girl move close, away from the driver. She glanced up at Mack, smiled at him. Mack barely shook his head and she stared through the window, all interest in Mack erased.

What in hell had he done by opening the passenger-side door and getting inside?

THE TRUCK SWERVED, the driver muscled it back on the road, a tire exploded and the vehicle with its passengers slid sideways into the road side, stuck the tire remains deep into thick, drying mud. The driver had the steering wheel for security; the girl bounced from the driver into Mack, who in turn hit the door hard enough the handle quit and Mack fell out, the girl landing on top of him.

"You there, you all right?" The question left Mack helpless with laughter. The girl pushed herself off Mack, using her hands to dig herself out of the mud. Mack struggled to sit up, the girl pushed her hands against him; "Go 'way, you're dirty."

Mack sat back in the mud and shook his head. The driver came around the front of the truck, careful not to get himself muddy. He looked at the busted tire, shook his head. "Mister, you know how to fix that damned tire?"

Mack quit laughing; he'd started with pebbles and a blue sky, with little understanding of what set him going. Now he was quiet. "Depends, what've you got for another tire. And a jack sure would help."

THE TIRE WAS changed, despite the truck's tilt into the mud, the girl's hysteria, and the driver's sullen attempts at helping. Mack's ultimate exhaustion was full blown at the end of four hours of miserable, back-breaking attempts and failures.

Back on the road, the girl sobbed until she realized no one cared, the driver stared through the windshield, paying no attention to his passengers. And Mack slept, head resting against the door frame, hands clenched together in his lap, mud drying on his filthy boots. As if those hands could ward off an evil the driver and his passenger did not see.

The house, in the small town of Cedar Grove, went back to the Oklahoma land rush. The main construction was sod and adobe, local material used to quickly set up a claim. Russell Nunn used the old house as his base; the farm itself was parcels of land joined together under the Nunn name. In the small world of the town and its environs, Russell Nunn was considered a wealthy and respected man. Lack of intelligence and a poor education had little to do with monetary respect.

Nunn parked the muddied truck near the barn. For a moment, the three truck inhabitants sat, motionless. Mack woke up in stages, and if Nunn and the girl had been aware, they would have seen flashes of pain cross the young man's face. What Mack suffered could be blamed on the effort to dig the truck out of the mud, change the tire – efforts that would challenge any man's ability and stamina. And they would have been right as well as wrong.

Nunn sighed, the girl patted her hair. "You can sleep in the barn. For now, come to the kitchen and you'll get fed." As he spoke, Russell Nunn remained staring at the barn door, refusing to look at his passenger.

The girl looked down and smiled. She could feel the struggle inside Mack as he came awake and seemed to understand where he was, and what he faced.

"This barn?" Nunn nodded; "There will be a cot for you. We keep it for sitting up with mares about to foal or...." Mack had stepped out of the truck, leaving Nunn to explain to himself.

The girl crawled out after Mack. They finally had time to look at each other. She was young, perhaps not twenty yet, with dark eyes and hair, smooth features until she smiled at Mack and he stepped back. The girl was herself, following no known measure of popular beauty. Her smile was enchanting, creating an unusual emotion in Mack. He wanted her to smile only for him.

Nunn' voice interfered; "She's my granddaughter, and lives with me and my wife.

THE BARN DID have a cot, placed in an unused stall. Made up with two blankets and an uncovered pillow. Nothing fancy; still it was a resting place, waiting for Mack. He sat down, hands trembling, his chest hurting. Tired, he thought, knowing a hidden truth and not wanting to see it. His private frailty that showed up in awkward moments; this time it was energy lost in a struggle with a perverse truck.

He laid himself out on the cot and again smiled; he'd been told to go to the house, the kitchen door, for food and drink. Right now he'd rather sleep.

ABRUPT

twenty-three

Left out on a tray, the thick sandwich, a small salad, a tall glass of water, a bowl of hot homemade vegetable soup with a big spoon was a mixture of scents and colors to tempt any palate. Yet the feast sat there on the kitchen table, the soup cooled, ice melted in the water, both the lettuce and the edges of bread darkened and rolled up, already stale, on the way to being spoiled.

Bonnie Nunn used the afternoon's stressful activity to get away from her grandparents and their continued concerns. It was bad enough she had to live with them. When Bonnie turned twenty-one she was leaving this wind-blown and desolate place and going out to live her own life.

Here in front of her, laid out for inspection was a promised meal not yet picked up for its intended use. The tray wasn't heavy and slipped easily through the back kitchen door. She made it to the barn with only a minor spill from the soup, leaving a wet spot on the tray edge.

Inside, she rested the tray on a closed trunk, and stood at the stall door, taking a moment to study the drifter Grandpa had picked up. Without this man's help, Bonnie knew they would never have gotten the truck free from the mud, and the tire changed.

Well he slept but he didn't snore. That was in his favor. And he didn't look special, sleeping like he was. Mouth open, breathing heavy as if it hurt. Bonnie had seen this man at work and there was a sense of wrong about him. Maybe he'd just gotten out of prison, or had done something bad and was running. Who else would be walking that miserable road into nowhere?

Oklahoma was an isolated prison compared to where she and her mother had lived before her mother disappeared. There was nothing left; she now lived with her grandparents, and no one spoke her mother's name, or had ever known the name of her father.

Here was a man, almost a boy from his looks, who was new and different. "Mister." Her voice was soft; "Mister." He rolled over and she could tell, by the tightening in his face, that the simple movement pained him. "Mister, I brought you some food."

At that, he sat up, very slowly and it wasn't pretty but he finally made it, feet planted firmly on the dirt floor, backside slung in the lumpy cot. He smiled briefly. "Ma'am, food's 'bout the only thing you could of said to get me moving." They were both quiet then; "It's 'bout that tray of food I can see from here." She was almost cross until a slow smile opened his face and she grinned in return.

ONLY THE PROSPECT of food could bring Mack out of the deep sleep. He knew, with a sigh, a sense of the inevitable, that life had shifted within him in the past hours. He intended to pay little attention to what he felt, for there was nothing to be done, no way to fix what was preordained. Mack knew that all the fuss and fury was helpless against what would happen, and too soon.

The consolation was simple; he knew, he'd known for over ten years now, what waited and oddly there was a freedom attached to that knowledge.

However, there were daily necessities that needed tending. And here was a sweet and unspoiled female offering him food. "Thank you, miss. Guess I was hungry after all. This afternoon...." She interrupted him; "Please, let's forget the mud and that...miserable vehicle my grandfather treasures."

Mack laughed; "Yes, ma'am." "Why are you laughing?" Mack thought about the question. "We get choices some times. Here, well, that mud-packed mess could be one or the other. Me, I'd rather laugh than be damned...sorry, miss."

A man to tell the truth; Bonnie wasn't certain she liked the trait, for the scattered remnants of her family rarely were this direct. Still, the bony, lean young man, whose hands trembled, who moved slowly with trouble, even as he smiled and joked, was a new part of life for her.

"Let me bring in the tray." She watched his face, saw the slightest tightening around the mouth, then the young man nodded, sighed, and spoke; "Please do. Me I'm mighty hungry."

THE FOOD WAS warm when meant to be chilled, or cold having started as hot; the bread tough at the edges, the odd choice of lettuce and a few vegetables that Mack didn't recognize, tasted like the most perfect food in all the world. Imperfections meant little; these tastes filled his empty belly, renewed his energy while hiding his ever-present weakness.

Sleep, good food, fresh water and Mack was alive again, not on the brink, at least for a little while. He grunted, and the girl looked at him. "The soup's good, miss. Thanks for bringing me the tray." No need for any deeper explanation. A simple, surface truth would do.

ONE TIME DURING the night, Mack woke up and sought out a crude and filthy toilet set to the back of the barn.

He woke again at ten in the morning. This time he lay on the cot, rested his head on crossed hands, freeing his chest, feeling the stronger, invasive tightness that would most likely kill him.

It didn't seem to matter.

A voice just outside had him grinning. "Mack, are you ready for coffee?" Just what he wanted so he sat up, with some difficulty. "Yes ma'am." Hopefully there would at least be a biscuit or two, maybe honey and butter. Or more.

But her grandfather came in, carrying a mug of creamed coffee and gave the cup and the biscuit to Mack. "She said to say good morning." Nothing more. Mack took a gulp and looked at the dry biscuit.

Mr. Nunn sighed; "What have you done to my granddaughter? She cannot stop talking about you. I don't like it." Mack took a bite of biscuit, gave him something to do while he thought how to answer the old man.

"Never mind. She's young. She'll learn." Nunn chewed his lower lip. "Boy, you want a job? Odd jobs in return for room and board, and maybe spending money. It'll keep you through the worst of the winter."

Mack finished the biscuit, drank the last of the coffee. Odd jobs, yeah. Life'd been filled with odd jobs.

"Sure."

twenty-four

A cold winter didn't come close to describing what blasted through Oklahoma that year; freezing rivers and pipes in houses, cracking insulated outside below-ground faucets.

Even with Russell Nunn giving Mack his cast-off winter clothes and springing for a new pair of warm winter boots, Mack usually came in to the warm corner of the barn half-froze and miserable. He even ended up with frost bite on one cheek and hands so damned cold he didn't dare put them near a fire.

Bonnie saw him, noticed the red marks on his face and knew exactly what to do. Her grandfather, of course, had taught her the signs, her grandmother showed her the dish filled water and the soft cloth, and the two women experimented on Mack's doubtful badges of honor.

It was a new and not very charming experience; Bonnie's touch was light on Mack's face. Hot water quickly turned cool against frozen skin; the resulting pain burned, then dissolved as Mack inhaled the girl's clean smell and relaxed. Even with the grandmother watching, Mack had to grin; this was a new piece to an odd life, one he was determined to enjoy.

The old woman pushed Bonnie to one side and plastered a white salve on those few gray places. Behind the old woman and her determined behavior, Bonnie smiled and Mack looked away. What he felt right then was in conflict with every moment behind him and he was scared. The sensation of warmth, of a tenderness rarely felt forced Mack to pull away, shut down his eyes, refuse the expression of emotion strangling him.

To remain aloof, distant from how he felt, Mack concentrated on the past; what he'd learned since he'd been told the truth. His father had been dismissed, Mack rarely thought of him, and never with any kindness. There were a few men, more women, who offered him the sanity of ease and affection.

Face to face, quite literally, with a young woman of some attraction and interest was beyond Mack's experience. In the past, he had of course run from any attraction. Now he could not leave, he couldn't even pull back or dismiss the girl.

The grandmother got up to add more hot water, Mack smiled, and the girl leaned forward and kissed him on the mouth. Mack jerked back, surprised even as he wanted more. It wasn't meant for him, even such a gentle touch aroused him. That much he recognized and as it made him warm, and wanted, it also was wrong. His entire life he'd been told to avoid such temptation. It would be lethal.

NOW HE KNEW. Inside his chest, his heart beat in an off-kilter rhythm and his lungs worked their own beat, leaving Mack unsettled and unstrung.

"Did you like that?" Her mouth moved in a sweet way, lips partly open, the edge of her tongue wetting the bottom lip. If Mack had enjoyed a young man's usual opportunities, he would know those signs, recognize her female experience. These small occurrences were a familiar move that told of her intentions, and Mack did not know that she'd learned such behavior through constant practice.

Mack leaned forward and caught her mouth, licked and nibbled what had been so long denied him.

"Young man, you will leave my granddaughter alone. Leave her, now!" Mack jerked away, the girl's mouth followed his until her grandmother's voice registered. Bonnie stood up, pushed at Mack as if refusing him.

NO ONE WAS fooled by her play-acting. Russell Nunn showed up accompanied by his angry wife, who spewed ugly accusations against Mack's innocence.

Bonnie went with her grandmother, not even looking back at Mack in apology. Mr. Nunn however, proved to be ferocious in defense of his granddaughter. Mack stood and accepted what the man said. As he listened, he also felt the girl's touch and knew an important part of his life had changed.

"YOU WILL LEAVE. When the cold breaks. I cannot in good conscience send you on the road now for you will freeze. However you will

stay in the barn, there will be no contact...."
Mack stopped listening. It took all his will to
keep standing. His body had changed, and
the new sensations were off-balance, his
senses confused. When he had time, Mack
realized the new sensations were a fire of
pleasure, nerve endings raw, too receptive to
a battalion of influence.

Licking his lips proved to be an intense
sensation. He'd been here before but never to
this degree. It was the pinnacle of male need
that Mack had never been allowed.

He studied Russell Nunn with a new
appreciation. The thought that this intense
pleasure was possible in each person both
aroused and amused him. What a huge effort
necessary to produce new members of any
species.

NUNN'S VOICAL COMMANDS ended with the
man demanding Mack agree to leave the girl
alone. It was an easy promise to give. Mack
had to keep himself from smiling; to the
concerned grandparents, what had occurred
between the two young people, had to have
been started by Mack. To believe their
beloved baby girl could be part of the
seduction was too much.

Mack found no difficulty in following
Nunn's protective direction. He lived in the
barn in warm isolation, ate the two meals a
day brought down by one of the hired man.

To keep from being too bored, Nunn
himself brought in broken harness, a three-
legged chair, and other items in need of

repair. If Mack was to be fed and protected, then he could earn the right by fixing broken items.

There was rightness in what Mack had been set to do. A broken man mending torn and broken material, unable to mend his own ailment. When he thought on it, the entire situation was turned sideways and backwards and he sat in damp barn carving a new leg or punching holes to attach separated leather and make a new rein.

EARLY IN MARCH, having spent six weeks in proper isolation, Mack learned from Mr. Nunn that tomorrow he, Mack, would be sent back out into the world. He would be driven in a general direction of Mack's choosing; wherever Mack wished to go, as long as the destination was outside the state of Oklahoma.

Actually packing carried a definite excitement; he was more than willing to move on and never look back.

There wasn't much to pack; socks, new underwear courtesy of Russell Nunn, boots, even a comb and toothbrush, and of all things a fresh razor.

He'd eaten a good meal of tough steak, vegetables and a baked potato, even a slice of lop-sided chocolate cake. And he'd taken a cup of hot tea outside, to sit and watch the sunset, the colors and clouds a reminder that soon enough spring would come.

When he came in, the barn was dimly lit, one kerosene lantern resting on a table near Mack's bed. Just enough light for him to do a wash-up. He studied the bed, knowing that tonight would be the last comfortable sleep he could count on.

She stood behind the cot, half-hidden in the shadows. There had been no further contact between them since that innocent kiss. Mack wasn't surprised, in fact he'd been wishing for this last moment.

She had come to him; he knew what could happen now, and despite what his weakness told him, he'd already decided. This was his chance, perhaps the only time and he would not deny himself the offered pleasure. There would be one experience he had not missed.

TWO PEOPLE COULD lie close on a narrow cot and the slender length of that bed allowed even more excuse for a man and a woman to touch intimate hidden places, delight in soft flesh pressed against rib and bone.

She wriggled herself under him, brought his hands up to her covered breasts and he knew enough to unbutton her dress and she arched her back, allowed one of his hands to slide under her and, with difficulty and false starts, helped him loosen the too-proper cotton and lace confinement. She lay back, breasts exposed. She sighed, he felt the softened flesh, then the rising, hardened nipples rested under his hands and his entire body shivered.

Her hands went between his legs and found him, hard, achingly ready. Her face lay

against his and Mack felt her smile. "You're
...I thought...." He couldn't stop now. Hips
raised, she unzipped him, brought him out;
erect, a bubble of fluid at the tip.

He knew what to do. Her skirt wrapped
around her waist, her panties pulled down,
hard enough they tore through one side as
Mack spread her legs and pushed himself
into her. Soft, fluid, flesh grabbing him, a give
and take he'd never known. He rose above
her, to go deeper, find more of these
incredible sensations.

Until he erupted, more and more fluid
jerking into her, emptying himself into warm
secretive flesh. Common sense told him not
to collapse on her but roll off, holding her
close, kissing her neck, her breasts, knowing
now that he would pay and he didn't care.

ABRUPT

True to his word, as if he did not know what his daughter had begun the night before, Russell Nunn drove Mack south and west from Guyman into the Texas panhandle, with a stop at Dalhart for a quick lunch before heading further south and west into New Mexico.

They exchanged no words; in fact after the poor lunch, Nunn had Mack ride in the back of the truck so there would be no chance for goodbyes or further explanations. For this poor kindness, Mack was relieved. He did not have to lie to the man, by refusing to answer indirect questions or resort to outright lies.

There was a break starting, an internal shift taking Mack to a different part of his remaining existence. Concentrating on what was left did no good, nothing would change except to weaken what had never been strong.

Nunn drove erratically, speeding down through the Texas panhandle, intent on getting Mack into New Mexico, where he felt he could leave the boy, with a clear conscience. Then he'd get on home and given time the affair between Bonnie and this disreputable drifter who had brought the girl to the edge of ruin, well the memory would fade and she would meet and marry a good man, one Russell Nunn and his wife accepted.

It didn't matter where; once they crossed over to New Mexico, Russell wanted the boy gone. Logan was as good as any place in New Mexico, whole damn state was cactus and chamisa and those stunted, twisted juniper come up from somewhere else. Seems like nothing wanted to stay in New Mexico. Russell grinned, no one could see him, that boy was hunched down in the truck bed, not hearing nothing but the wind.

Seems that even the State of New Mexico really didn't want this boy, Mack, though Russell was sure that wasn't the boy's real name.

It was simple; stop the truck outside of town, still on a decent road, let the boy out give him $50 in small bills and get turned around, head back to civilization and Oklahoma.

MACK DIDN'T WATCH the truck turn and head north and east. He stared down at the wad clenched in his left hand. Fifty dollars; he'd rarely seen that much. Felt like indecent betrayal money, for past indiscretions, so recent that Mack could smell her, feel her softness. The thought of what he'd done shamed him even now; no one looking, no one to care. Or listen to his confusion, explanation or dismissal.

In a recess of his mind where only certain memories were kept, he smiled when he thought of Bonnie Nunn and her special, unexpected generosity. It was how Mack chose to remember his brief time in Oklahoma.

Meanwhile he was presented with the next segment of an endless journey. A sign said 'Logan' but Mack saw only a few buildings, a lean-to holding two mules and a pregnant mare, symbols of a different century. The land could be anywhere, scrub brush and blowing dirt. Water came from a flat-turning wheel held high in a rough-looking frame.

He'd not been here before even as the land was familiar. Looking south, he chose to follow the dirt road. He'd come from the north so south and maybe west could be the next answer.

Half a mile down a road, through what passed for a village, Mack stopped. He could take only a few shallow breaths and his entire chest hurt, as if fire lived inside him.

TEN YEARS AND nothing had changed. The internal pain, erratic heart, an expected death sentence for him, to be buried with his baby brothers. Here and now, more life lived than ever promised or expected. Not much by other standards, but for him, the smell of dusty air, hard work, even chasing cattle from the back of a horse or changing a muddy tire; all simple ordinary moments he'd never been promised or thought they could become his.

Ten years; he wasn't sure where he'd started, too young to know or care. Anger at what was left of a family, a town with no name, paying too much attention to his anger at the cheating life handed him. But he knew instinctively that somewhere in this dry, unpromising land there was a small cemetery with two identical gravestones and he needed to visit this place. More than likely no one paid much attention or that the land had been taken, the few tiny bones, a last name scraped on roughed rock, would mean nothing.

It was for Mack, born as Henry Miles Lawson, to find these few remnants and honor them.

His lungs had settled, the clamor of his beating heart was steady. He had fifty dollars and didn't need much else. It was for Mack to find a future, starting with learning from his past. He smiled, raised his head to the sun, took a deep breath and began the last leg of his journey.

REMOTE AND INDIFFERENT, Mack knew the ground he walked was roughed by blowing wind, bare down to rock, few clumps of grass high enough to trip Mack if he wasn't careful. When he stumbled and had to fight for balance, Mack actually laughed. To be defeated passively by bumps and rocks; as if he'd ever traveled over smooth ground.

The land showed no difference from too many other places. Ten years as a stranger blurred lines, houses, barns, derelict buildings, none of these landmarks stirred Mack's memory. Still he walked, sleeping on hard ground, digging spoiled food out of trash cans, accepting a meal from a housewife needing simple work.

Each day was a disappointment, each step Mack took eroded another piece of precious time. He walked straight south, not looking but listening, waiting for a sign. Eventually he went west, along a thin stream simply to have water near him.

The deep skin on one cheek, that had been winter frost-bite, was now a slow peeling of dead tissue. Going from a dark burn to dead white, the areas sloughed off in small pieces, which Mack absent-mindedly picked apart, until his face hurt and he knew what he'd been doing.

Thankfully he could not see his own destruction. Energy was needed to regrow his face, and conditions were not strong enough for a rebirth.

He slept, napping in mid-day, finding a tree or brush for shade, letting himself drift into a quiet peace.

A farmer, tinkering with a broken harrow, asked for Mack's help which he gladly gave, at least familiar with the piece, able to hold and bend while the farmer repositioned several screws. The patch held, the two men stood back to admire what they'd accomplished. But when the farmer offered a dry bed and a few meals in payment, Mack smiled and said no, he had to find a place and hadn't reached it yet.

DRIFTING, WITHOUT ANY time, except for moving during the early sun, sleeping mid-day, walking again until it was dark; Mack's time was limitless, only the lack of food kept him slowed, until his body accepted the reduction of fuel, and Mack continued his journey based on what he could scavenge.

Walking took him near the small gathering of buildings, called Clovis. The area almost seemed familiar. He entered the town, paid out a few of his precious dollars for a simple meal, a cup of coffee, with refills and a smile from the hurried waitress. He'd been a child when he'd been here and it wasn't home. Even so there was a sense here of the past that gave Mack hope.

He asked, and the waitress had time enough to lean over the counter, stare at Mack in a manner that make him uncomfortable; "Yeah, folks come into town for supplies, sometimes for a court case. There's farms to the west, don't know much about them. Only got recognized as a county ten years ago. It's a new world down here. We're goin' places, you can bet on that." She rambled on, gossip and half-knowledge as if she used words to keep Mack's attention.

He abruptly stood, thanked her, paid the bill and left a quarter as a tip, then left. Now he had a direction; it did not occur to him to recognize the waitress and her surprised look.

ABRUPT

twenty-six

The diner food didn't stay with him for long. Kneeling to vomit surprised him; bent over, spewing rough meatloaf and canned green beans, Mack recognized a new frailty. Food no longer supported him, his body could not accept nourishment. Water salved Mack's throat, even the brackish, sand-filled water trickling through a wide arroyo.

He stood, covered his mess with the edge of his boot, moving sand and rock to hide the poor human remnants. His journey meant nothing except to him, giving him a reason to keep going.

There was a dirt track crossing the arroyo, Mack followed the erratic intrusion of tire marks, gouges left by horses, deep clefts in old mud that would belong to nameless machines. The trail followed the arroyo along the top, skirting small groups of thin pines and twisted juniper. He could see tips of houses, flat roofed, peaked barns, even burned out fields.

Around a bend, at an angle to the disappearing arroyo, were the charred remains of a barn next to the outline of what had been a house. Mack could see few remnants of what had been farm machines, even recognizable implements; a pitch fork missing one tine, broken off and never replaced. A heavy barn sweeper now lopsided from fire, one end charred, the other end looking unused.

Nothing special, no identifying marks of who might have made these utilitarian instruments except that they were not manufactured and sold, they'd been hand-done, with skill and affection, and they stopped Mack's journey.

He sat, on a rock slab once pulled from the ground, set back so a road could continue with traffic. He was grateful for the rock; his tired body allowing him to lean on his arms for support, while he studied the blackened remains and considered what drew him to their insignificant and casual display.

AN OLD MAN, first identified by the mismatched sound of his walk, then by the bent shadow and finally the figure appeared in front of Mack. He had to look up and the eager face of the old man made him briefly smile.

A hard-worked woman joined the talk and the husband and wife filled in part of what Mack assumed. There had been confusion about his current name, which the old man insisted on, wanting obviously to soothe Mack by not using the childhood name and finally the old woman relented. He was Mack, never again to be Henry Miles Lawson.

He learned too much and not enough. Yes this had been where his father ended life; a new wife, a new farm, old hand-made farm items. Then only sadness and a terrible end. Fire, death, buried among strangers with land sold out of the family. Those who took

Mack in for the night did not even know the first name of his father's second wife, nor were either of them sure where the Lawsons had been buried.

Despite years and miles, Mack felt a tentative letdown in how and when his father died. For all the years of being gone, Mack had kept the old man alive, never letting him age or change in his way of life.

Now he faced an unwanted and unexpected truth. The object of those exiled years, the impossibility of going home despite his original decision to leave, had always been a distant, last choice, and now Mack learned that just after he'd left, the world behind him disappeared and the changes meant what he'd thought was a safety net dissolved. Lost finally in a fire, with a woman whose name Mack would never know.

TWO OLD PEOPLE, married for fifty years, hard-working, with a simple faith in the goodness of their life, offered Mack home-grown food, which he could barely keep down, and the blessing of a safe bed. Early the next morning, Mack heard the woman approach the back room since it was time for Mack to be up and at work.

Then he barely heard the old man's voice, telling his wife to leave the boy alone, let him sleep. Young Lawson was tired, any fool could see that.

To hear himself called 'Lawson' reopened a long-covered wound in Mack. He rolled over and went back to sleep, knowing even as he drifted off that 'Lawson' no longer existed.

He woke later with no sense of time and god-awful hungry. Sitting in their neatened kitchen, however, Mack found he couldn't eat much. He lifted his head, listened to the old woman, and stared at the walls, while he drank a glass of juice.

The old woman put out a jar of grape jelly and out of misplaced kindness, Mack spooned the dark purple jelly thick onto the bread, finding he enjoyed the experience of home-made jelly, as much as he could want, spread on freshly-made slices of bread.

Next to the stove was a spattered calendar, its headline promoting the local feed store. Mark leaned back while chewing on the bread and jam, surprised by the date. He'd paid little attention over the years, except when he remembered his own birthday. The calendar said it was October, maybe the middle of the week. The year was 1929. Another year, he thought, another marker in others' lives. Where he could feel a deeper, more lethal dissolution within his fading systems. He only needed a few more months.

HE HEADED NORTH, this time fortified with a half-cup of coffee heavily laced with frothy new milk. He thanked the couple, as they stood next to each, taking comfort from the other's flesh.

They did not push to feed him, they seemed to know that what they'd done was enough, even as the past twelve hours had taken little from them except to offer kindness and the illusion of safety to a wearied drifter. A kindness they would never fully understand, nor would they care.

Watching the young man leave, carrying a bedroll and sundries across his back, with an old jacket tied to his waist, a hat so filthy that even the husband would not wear it, the two looked at each other.

"He never ate 'nough to keep him goin'. Wish I could have done more, Martin." "Had what he needed, Irene. He'll find the loaf of bread you stuck in that roll. He won't care it was yesterday's bakin'. Don't think being stale's gonna bother him. Ain't no one gettin' that boy to eat what he didn't want. Wish I had better news for him. But he took it well, and now, I don't know. He's headed north, where they came from." They sighed together.

"Best get back to work. That hay won't be cuttin' itself. Give me a kiss."

twenty-seven

Going north. Each step taken felt more and more familiar. I hoped it wasn't my imagination but a reality I'd misplaced. Since there was no memory of my parents, not even a sense left of my father or any idea of his second wife, I held the good folks I'd just left as an ideal I could accept. Irene and Martin were simple people, not like some of those I'd met and then left behind. They could not be my family, that much I knew, but they did stand out as an example of what I might have had.

I was going north to find where I'd been born. No name came to mind, and no one had a name to tell me. So many places alive for a short time and then abandoned. Small village like Smithtown, or Currierville; names no longer defining where people once lived. There might be a road, or an old school, the remains of a tired town building, but the life making a place a home had long been abandoned.

There was no road map or directions to lay out and study, and decide on which trail might lead to a crossroads or an abandoned cellar, a rotted and collapsed corral, a small marker close to the ground with incised numbers having no more meaning.

All this was difficult enough even as I realized the thread tying me to a strange life was unraveling. I'd never seen them, but what I truly was seeking were those two small, worn tombstones, bearing faded names and dates, hidden now by new-growth trees, and a barrenness of life. Abandoned houses, collapsed barns; fields left to grow weeds, springs dried up, filled with drifted, blown dust.

All this is what I envisioned as I kept walking, even as I felt a slow collapse of every tissue. Only determination kept me moving.

THERE WERE TOO many foundations hidden by overgrowth, single leaning posts once part of a fence line or corral. Even the skeleton of a tired barn, shorn of its board covering, holding nothing but a blowing wind. Mack knew of the hard times behind him, where drought and high sun, lack of rain, had worn out farms and ranches, even buried beneath the shifted earth once-vital springs or streams.

He kept walking in spite of what he should know; he would not give in to doubt now, he wanted to see for himself, even if it was only a few boards, the trace of four corners and the sliding wood that had once been a door. Returning to a place left blank in the mind, not even reduced to a memory, was in itself as futile and brief as Mack's life had been and would soon become. Not recorded or kept, in a family bible or a box in an attic; the trace of a few lost moments mattering to no one.

Walking was what he knew and would have to remember. The vision remained unfocused and ahead of him; two small graves. He would not be added to this lonely place for there would be no one to bury him. In an odd, vague manner, Mack embraced what had to come. He did not want to die in a public bathroom or lie frozen in a cheap boarding room until a smell alerted other occupants, that somewhere, someone else had died.

That night, while going through his bedroll before settling for sleep, Mack discovered the old woman's parting gift, a day-old loaf of bread. He couldn't help smiling; such a kindness pleased him. And despite the crust being tough, he chewed contentedly, savoring the salt/sweetness even as he thought of those old people who would offer up such a homely, common-place item.

TO GET UP the next morning was a slow, painful struggle, out of keeping with Mack's activities. He gnawed on the remaining loaf, sipped at metallic water he'd carried in a screw-top bottle, then waited to allow the basic nutrition work on sore muscles.

As he began another day of walking, Mack began to realize he no longer saw the empty land, the stunted trees, deep arroyos or smooth and vast grassland, now tipped with bursting seed, and offering an abundance that was in fact a lie. There were few cattle, little nutrition in the crop, no place to sell it, and no rain in sight.

None of this seemed to matter. Mack walked, eyes down, then stopping to raise his head and look around.

ABRUPT

Now there was the shape of a small store a half-mile ahead. Only remnants of abandoned buildings surrounded the store. As Mack got closer, he saw a hand-lettered sign proclaiming the almost useless building as 'Two Stone" and there weren't stones, except for pebbles and scattered gravel. Mack grinned at the absurdity; folks never changed.

Despite signs of an empty interior, Mack went in, carrying 37 cents in his left hand and intent on buying at least canned meat or tinned sausages.

One man sat leaning back in a ragged chair. He barely looked up; "You need anything?"

Shelves almost bare, dust on the dried floor boards, no one else in the store. "I need a can of meat, if you've got it." With no fanfare, the man shakes his head. "We got nothing here, mister."

The voice nudged Mack's recall. "Mr. Sutton?" The two men studied each other. The so-called store keeper lifted one eyebrow in silent query. Mack was definite; "Mr. Sutton, I know you. At least I did. Once."

BITS AND PIECES" flashed through him. The store had been active; people came and went into the post office side, where Mrs. Sutton handed out mail and gossip and an occasional stamp.

Mack remembered.

"YOU'RE THAT BOY what run away. Your daddy he sure was mad. Right to the middle of puttin' in crops. I remember you. Your pa he went on 'bout you and you bein' no...." The man then had the grace to shut up.

After a long silence, then man looked straight at Mack. "Don't look so good, kid. Guess life on the road wasn't up to your standards."

Mack sighed, some people never changed, and he remembered this man picking on Mack and his family, or what was left after the two boys died and the mother left. He wasn't kind then, and hadn't changed since.

"When the town up and blew away, your pa, you know he got himself a woman, don't think they married. Anyway the old man he leaves that useless farm and goes south. One of my best customers."

It wasn't difficult not to laugh. 'Best customer'. And oddly Mack found he didn't like it that the man remembered him. Still he would not offer any defense to the storekeeper. If that was how the man still saw himself.

"Canned meat, if you've got it. Or sausages would do."

THEY PARTED IN silence, Mack having given up his last few pennies in trade for a dusty can of those damned sausages. Leaving the store was a relief even if it meant more walking. Mack felt he could find what he wanted, even if it took a day or two. He'd

ABRUPT

come to a place he'd been as a child. The disparity of the richness when he was young and the devastation that had ruined lives, saddened too many who saw the wind and dry blow away their dreams.

twenty-eight

Walking again, stumbling over crumbling ruts, stepping carefully around exposed rocks and cholla, wanting desperately to lie down and sleep but it wasn't time yet. Mack panted from the day's heat as he moved. There was nothing to remind him, no house, barn, animals, even the fields were barren, weeds growing where there had been hay and cattle.

He was tired, reaching into himself to keep moving. Always moving. A thin tree offered shade and Mack changed his angle of direction. The field was bumpy, roughened through misuse; Mack stumbled then picked up his feet.

There was a gate attached to the solitary tree. It was hooked to a single post, and the heavy wooden gate sagged, in places touching the ground. There was no more fence, only the tall post nailed to the single tree, and a receptive post looking isolated and useless.

He hung the bedroll on the gate, then removed his hat and had the pleasure of placing it on the isolated gate post, stepping back to admire his new surroundings.

From where he stood, he could see in every direction; unused roads, dilapidated uninhabited houses, partial corrals. And weeds. Still, the land was growing low levels of grass, even the few trees had a green tinge of new leaves.

ABRUPT

He sat, the old jacket beside him, back against the taller gate post, and opened the can of tinned sausage. Using his knife, he speared the meat, didn't look as he put a link in his mouth. Not a bad taste, so he had two more links before he got tired again. Only late morning, sun not yet overhead, and he was exhausted. Looking around, at the peace, quiet, and no one watching, he rolled over on his side, wadded the old jacket under his head, and slept.

A RAVEN WOKE him, looking down from the twisted tree. Having been quiet so Mack could have a good sleep, the raven was bored and decided to make a racket. Mack rolled over and opened his eyes, picked up a clump of grass and dust and threw it up, missing the raven who flew off in disgust.

Lying flat on his back gave Mack a different view of the land. It took a few minutes for what he was seeing to make any sense. They were few, some fenced in, other almost lost in the dried grass, but what they were made him sit up.

Tombstones, some broken, lying in pieces across a raised area which would be an old grave. Stones stood close together, others were broken monuments, standing in magnificent isolation. Farther from the gate, with no defining lines, tombstones stood in rigid formation, as if ordered to lie there in remembrance of those who had died.

Barely breathing, Mack stood, held to the tall gate post, let himself settle, then

174

walked through the useless gate and began to explore what had been left behind.

He was lost in reading the epitaphs, names and dates, most of them from 1880 to the end of WWI. A few were soldiers who had died later, from their wounds overseas. Three were soldiers who died in the flu epidemic of 1918, young men forced together in military posts, where germs and poor sanitation created a breeding ground.

Mack read these names and dates and sometimes the cause of death, and he found himself indifferent. Not unsympathetic to the memorial to those who died, but it was an impersonal regret.

Then, as he had hoped but did not want to see them, there were two small stones, crude writing chipped into the smoothed rock.

They were his brothers. Mack dropped to his knees and balanced himself on his left hand, allowed his right hand to touch and follow the chipped names.

Both of them said 'Henry Miles Lawson." One bore the date of 1894, the other was 1896. Year of birth for each child, year of death only a few months later. Neither child lived a full year.

The third and last Henry Miles Lawson sat back on his haunches, bowed his head, and very softly mourned for the remains of two infant brothers he never knew.

ABRUPT

EPILOGUE

In the early 1950s, land became valuable, even in the southwestern states, including New Mexico. Great slices of land were bought up and broken into smaller sections which developers sold to those wanting to 'live in the country.' Interestingly enough, many of these potential country dwellers found that despite loving the freedom of the great outdoors, they also want the conveniences of a more modern town.

Tarred roads, electricity, a refrigerator, and either an electric or gas stove. Even a washing machine and a vacuum cleaner became necessities to these country dwellers.

Eventually the land dealers approached the old cemetery, now completely overgrown; the gate and two fence posts had fallen in and disappeared, lost in weeds and bushes, and the juniper and piñon trees.

The developers researched old records before digging up and moving the conventional graves, and when they found no living relative of those who were buried, they simply gathered up the bones and reburied them in a group at the back of a nearby town graveyard.

Much to the developers' surprise, a collection of scattered bones and shredded bits of clothing was found above ground, near the puzzling two stones, where the hand-carved names were identical although the dates were several years apart. No one of that particular last name could be found, so the bones of two small infants were included with the scattered adult bones, minus the skull. There were a few scattered rags; the remains of a shirt, old torn jeans and leather soled boots, which when picked up disintegrated into dust and small pieces.